THE ESTATE

a novel

MARTIN KING

MAINSTREAM
PUBLISHING

EDINBURGH AND LONDON

085494163

First published in Great Britain in 2001 by
MAINSTREAM PUBLISHING COMPANY (EDINBURGH) LTD
7 Albany Street
Edinburgh EH1 3UG

ISBN 1 84018 410 8

A catalogue record for this book is available from the British Library

Typeset in Gill Sans and Lithos
Printed and bound in Great Britain by Cox & Wyman Ltd, Reading, Berkshire

CONTENTS

ONE	**The Grand Opening**	7
TWO	**The Singhs**	11
THREE	**Lynn**	25
FOUR	**Justin and Tony**	37
FIVE	**Terry the Cabbie**	49
SIX	**Take Me Back Home**	63
SEVEN	**Tinkers and Travellers and Troublemakers**	75
EIGHT	**Nigel's Nightmare**	87
NINE	**Where Did it All go Wrong?**	101
TEN	**Fix My Car**	111
ELEVEN	**Grass**	123
TWELVE	**The Tavern on the Green**	135
THIRTEEN	**A Season's Greeting**	171

ONE

THE GRAND OPENING

The sky was cloudless, clear and blue. The sun was shining and although for once it was a hot day, there was a nice cooling breeze to go with the carnival atmosphere. A twenty-piece brass band played away up on the stage, which had been decorated with ribbons, balloons and banners. The sound of children laughing and screaming and having fun came from the many fairground rides and side stalls, where you could have the thrill of your life, win a coconut or hook a plastic duck, or take home a goldfish in a see-through plastic bag. Excited kids crowded around to see what their friends had won. A group of Mods hanging around the bumper cars listening to The Who sing about their generation took the piss out of a Teddy boy in his drape suit and winkle-picker shoes as he walked past with his girlfriend. Near them a gang of Rockers in leather jackets, with matching oily hair and jeans, screwed at a mob of Skinheads with shaved heads, who were competing to see who could hit the punch ball the hardest for a penny a time. One rolled up the sleeves of his button-down shirt, pulled his red braces from his shoulders and let them dangle around his jungle-green army trousers before hitting the ball with all his might. The others mocked and laughed at him as the dial registering the power of the punch hardly moved. The skinhead's steel toe-capped boot connected with a younger boy's arse. 'Don't laugh at me, cunt,' he snarled.

A football match with about thirty-a-side was taking place on the far side of the field. The kids had put jumpers down as goalposts and seemed to be oblivious to the pomp and ceremony going on around them. 'GOAL!' half of them roared as the ball sailed into the air, over the fence and into the allotments where a couple of old boys, bent double, raked the earth and chatted about this year's crop of cabbages, seemingly oblivious to the rest of the world as they tended their pride and joy.

The Mayor's black limousine drove across the grass and pulled up slowly next to the stage, where two young boys aged about six sat, each sucking on an orange-flavoured frozen Jublee, the juice running down their arms and trickling onto the wooden steps. Out of the limousine jumped two men in dark glasses and black suits. They shooed the boys away and looked around, scanning the crowd before opening the car doors. The man himself stepped out, the thick gold ceremonial chain that hung from his neck nearly touching the waistband of his trousers. Just the council's luck that the person in office this year was only a couple of inches short of being a midget. The chain looked ridiculous. On a normal-sized mayor it would have looked all right, but on Snow White's little helper it seemed disproportionately huge.

The band struck up 'Rule Britannia', though no one knew what that had to do with the Mayor, now climbing the steps onto the stage. A few dignitaries and selected guests, family and friends were seated in a cordoned off area at the front of the stage.

Dressed in their Sunday best, they smiled and clapped politely as the town crier announced the arrival of the Mayor. The band then went on to play 'We All Live in a Yellow Submarine'. 'Why have all the songs got a nautical theme to them?' asked a puzzled reporter from the local rag. 'Because,' answered one of the Mayor's aides, 'The Mayor's father was a decorated officer in the Royal Navy, and the Mayor himself is a keen sailor. He is the commodore of a yacht club on the south coast, and he also takes a keen interest in his local sea cadet group.'

With his wife smiling at his side, the Mayor adjusted the mike stand and welcomed everyone to the grand opening of the estate. It wasn't the real opening of the estate, since all the tenants had already moved into the flats some weeks previously. Today was an excuse for the council to waste some more of the ratepayers' money, a sort of glorified piss-up for the chosen few. The Mayor waffled on about this estate being the future of all estates across the whole country, and how privileged he was to be part of the celebrations. This council would lead, he went on, and the others would follow. This was to be a multi-cultural housing development of the modern age, and the 1960s would be remembered in years to come for its values of peace and friendship, which would be the basis for people of all colours, creeds and religions to live side by side in harmony.

Finally the Mayor ended his speech. 'Now,' he said, 'it is time to cut the ribbon and open our brand-new community centre.' The band struck up 'Ferry across the Mersey' as he stepped down from the stage to a ripple of applause and, followed by his entourage, strode across the grass to the main doors of the community centre. A pair of scissors was handed to him by one of his lackeys and he snipped the royal-blue piece of ribbon in two. 'I declare this centre and the estate officially open,' he smiled, and the photographers' cameras flashed.

THE ESTATE

'Fuck off inside, you short-arsed little wanker!' shouted one of the lads from the football team, who were standing outside the Tavern pub drinking and larking about in the warm sunshine. 'Fuck off back to the circus, you dwarf,' shouted another red-faced drinker. The crowd cheered and laughed, and the Mayor was quickly surrounded by his suited security men and half-led and half-pushed by them inside the centre, where entry that day was by invitation only. Two commissioners in full regalia stood guard on the door. Once the Mayor's party were safely inside, the outside world was shut out and the celebrations continued.

People began to drift off. A council truck pulled up and the workers began to dismantle the stage and sweep up the mounds of litter, happy because they were being paid double time. Bad light forced the kids to finish their football match and they picked their jumpers up from the piles they'd used as goalposts and wearily headed home. The sun went down and was lost for the day behind one of the six drab grey concrete twenty-storey tower blocks. On the estate there were also a dozen smaller three-storey blocks and some three-bedroom houses and low-level bungalows. The greens in between the buildings were well manicured and the colourful flowerbeds were in bloom. The day was all but over, but their new lives were about to begin for the inhabitants of the estate.

TWO

THE SINGHS

'Go on, get out of my shop and never come back.'

'Fuck off you Paki cunt!' came the reply. 'Fuck off back to your own country and take your smelly family with ya.'

'Out, out, out!' shouted Mr Singh, his voice stuttering with anger as he showed the two small boys the door. 'Bloody thieves.'

'Morning Mr Singh.'

'Morning Miss Smith,' replied Mr Singh as he gathered his composure.

'I see them boys are giving you more trouble.'

'I'm seriously thinking about buying a guard dog,' said Mr Singh, 'maybe a Dobermann or an Alsatian, just something to let would-be thieves know we have some protection.'

Mr Singh had run the local shop and post office since the opening of the estate. He and his wife were simply known by their surnames there, as their first names were deemed unpronounceable to the locals. When the Singhs had first moved in they'd invited their family and friends to a celebratory housewarming party. It had been a lovely evening, but when the Singhs went out to wave their guests off afterwards they discovered that many of their cars had been vandalised – tyres had been let down or slashed, radio aerials had been broken and bent, and paintwork was scratched.

He had scrimped and saved, begged and borrowed the money to open this new shop unit and move into the flat above, where he lived with his wife, their two children and his elderly parents. Mr Singh and his parents had arrived in Britain from a small village about a hundred miles north of Delhi in India in the mid-'50s and had settled in Leicester, in the Midlands. Mr Singh's mum had worked as a nurse for the National Health Service for nearly fifteen years and his father had been an ambulance man for the same amount of time. Mr Singh, an only child, grew up in the Midlands until he moved to London, where he was introduced at an arranged meeting to a shy, small-framed girl who later became his wife. He helped out in his wife's father's textile business in Hounslow, West London after his move.

The couple lived with her parents until their two children, Sukhdev and Manjit came along, and they saved up the deposit for a rented flat. When the chance to start up their own business on the estate came along they raised the money and took the plunge, but racial ignorance ran deep in these parts and some of the local kids, following the example of their parents and grandparents, had no time for the Singh family. They thought only one thing – that blacks and Asians had no place on the estate.

Mr Singh's children were both at private school, and they rarely mixed with kids in the local area. Education was an important thing in the Singh household. Sukhdev was almost fourteen and excelled at his studies. He was good at every subject and also captained the under-sixteen hockey team. He was accepted at school, where he was popular with fellow pupils and teachers alike; the colour of his skin didn't come into it. But since moving to the estate, two things made him stand out – his red-and-grey striped blazer and his brown face. The very first day, on arriving home from school, he was called names and chased by a gang of kids as he stepped off the bus, which luckily for him stopped right outside the parade of shops where his dad's post office was. Not a good start to a new life in a new area, at a new address. He began to wonder if he would ever be happy there.

Sukhdev's sister Manjit was a year younger than him and academically she was even brighter. She loved to study every spare minute of the day and could always be found with her nose stuck in a book – she hoped to get the A levels she needed to get into university and study medicine. Her ambition was to go one step further than her grandmother; Manjit wanted to train in the National Health Service, qualify as a doctor and then go abroad and work in Africa, or maybe India. She dreamed of doing some good in the world.

Mr Singh was working one afternoon stacking packets of cigarettes and boxes of matches onto the shelves when the glass front door of the shop burst open and Sukhdev stumbled in. He collapsed in a heap on the floor sending crisps, sweets and tins of dog food flying in every direction. As he landed his pursuers stood outside, looking in through the door and laughing. He picked himself up before his father could reach him, brushed himself down and checked his clothes to make sure they were not ripped or torn – the last thing he wanted was his father to be cross about a damaged uniform. He had worked so hard to pay for his son's school blazer.

'Are you all right there, son? What's going on?' Mr Singh asked.

THE ESTATE

'Nothing, Dad,' said Sukhdev as he bent down and began putting the tins back on the shelves with one hand and righting an upturned box of crisps with the other. One of the crisp packets had split open, and as he held his fingers to his nose he could smell cheese and onion.

'Sukhdev, what has happened?' Mr Singh bent down to help his son tidy up.

'Nothing Dad, just a few kids thinking they're having a laugh,' he said as he peeled the remains of a Mars Bar from the sole of his shoe. Through the shop window he could see the backs of the gang who had chased him disappearing into a block of flats opposite.

'Do you want me to go after them, son?'

'And do what?' asked Sukhdev. 'Make matters worse? If you were to go after them, they would only go and get their older brothers or even their dads. Leave it Dad, I can look after myself.'

Sukhdev had certainly inherited the Sikh fighting spirit of his forefathers. His name in Punjabi meant 'calmness'. His father had told him many stories of the great fighting men and warriors of the Punjab, how they had battled with and repelled Muslim raiders from the north. He told him about the five Ks, the five physical symbols adopted by Sikhs: the Kesh, the long, uncut hair worn under the turban; the Kara, a steel bracelet worn on the wrist or arm; the Kirpam, a ceremonial sword worn sheathed on the waistband; the Kanga, a comb to keep the uncut hair tidy; and the Kaccha, the long-john style undergarment which must not come below the knee. The Sikhs were a proud race. Although Mr Singh and his wife were brought up in the traditional religious way by their parents, he and his wife would let Sukhdev and his sister decide if they wanted to follow the old ways. Sukhdev was now at an age where he could, if he wished, grow his hair long and wear a turban, for the Sikh religion states that when a boy is old enough to grow a beard he may wear a turban if he chooses.

That night in bed, Mr Singh tossed and turned, unable to get to sleep. When they'd first moved in a group of skinheads had come into the shop late one evening and had tried pinching some cans of beer. Mr Singh had stood up to them and told them to put the stuff they'd hidden inside their jackets back. 'We ain't got nothing,' one of them had said. 'Prove it,' taunted another. Mr Singh had grabbed one of the boys and pulled open the front of his jacket. Cans of light ale fell to the floor and in the struggle the boy went backwards into the shelves, tripped and landed on top of the frozen foods cabinet. He had picked himself up and run off with the rest of them. Half an hour later, one of the boy's dads, along with his uncle, had appeared in the shop. Mr Singh was standing behind the counter.

'I've come here about my boy,' said the man. 'I understand you assaulted him.'

'Assaulted him?'

' Yes,' said the lad's father, 'he tells me he was in here with his mates buying some booze to take to a party when you jumped on him and ripped the cans from his hands.'

Mr Singh shook his head in disbelief. 'How old is your son?'

'Fourteen.'

'Then first of all, why are you allowing him to drink beer, knowing he's under-age, and second, coming in here and standing up for him when he's been caught red-handed pinching it?'

The two men looked at one another. 'Touch him again and you'll have me to answer to.'

'Yeah,' said the other man as they walked out of the shop with a parting shot of 'You shouldn't even be in this country.'

THE ESTATE

'What's up?' whispered Mr Singh's wife, interrupting his thoughts.

'It's Sukhdev,' he said, turning to face her in the dark. 'It's those boys, they're making his life a misery and if he's not happy, then how can this family be happy? If you call the police they tell you they will send someone round, and that someone nine times out of ten, never turns up until the following day. When I ring again, they say that if my son's not been touched then there is nothing they can do.'

'We'll talk about it tomorrow, let's get some sleep now,' said Mrs Singh. Mr Singh lay awake for a long time, listening to his wife's steady breathing as she fell into a deep sleep. He had just dozed off when he was woken by banging and shouting on the front windows of the shop. 'Fuck off back home Pakis.' There was laughter, and then silence as the voices disappeared into the night. He looked at the alarm clock next to the bed – 2 a.m. The adults had taken over from the kids.

The next morning, as they did every morning, either Mr Singh or his wife would take it in turns to make the kids breakfast and sit with them and chat while the other worked downstairs in the shop. This particular morning Grandpa looked after the shop while Mum, Dad and Grandma sat round the kitchen table. Mr Singh poured himself a cup of tea from the pot that stood in the centre. He took a sip and then, looking at everyone present, he pushed the *Exchange and Mart* weekly paper to one side. His search for a dog would have to wait.

'Is everyone happy?' he asked.

'What sort of a question is that?' replied Mrs Singh.

'Well, we've only been here a month and certain things, well, certain things have happened.' Mr Singh was trying to choose his words carefully. 'Look what happened yesterday with Sukhdev.'

Before he could say another word, his son jumped to his feet.

'Sit down,' said Mrs Singh.

Sukhdev obeyed. 'Dad, what happened yesterday was partly my fault. I should never have put myself in that position.'

'Sukhdev,' replied his dad, 'you were coming home from school. How is that putting yourself in a position?'

Mrs Singh buttered some toast and looked around at the silent faces. 'Let's forget what's happened and put it down to ignorance on the part of a small minority of the people on the estate. The majority of our customers are courteous and polite. It's the people who don't use the shop who seem to have a problem with us being here. Look at your Uncle Gurnham and the problems he had when he opened the first Indian restaurant in Southall, back in the late 1950s. Teddy boys would come and cause trouble. They'd turn over the tables and chairs, throw food about and run off without paying. But slowly, very slowly, he built the business up, until soon you had to book to get a table. In the end some of the people who had caused trouble in the past began to come back as regular customers. Uncle Gurnham went from strength to strength. Soon he opened another restaurant, followed by another and then another, and he became a very rich man.'

'So what Mum is saying,' said Mr Singh, 'is that it's early days, so let's stick with it and find the light at the end of the tunnel.'

The children looked at Grandma, who gave them one of her sweet, reassuring smiles. She stood up, straightened her blue and gold sari and said something to Mr Singh in Punjabi. They both laughed. 'Come on kids,' said Mr Singh, looking in the mirror as he brushed his beard and fiddled with his white turban, 'get your things together, I'll run you to school in the car.

THE ESTATE

I've got to go to the warehouse, so I'll drop you both off at school.'

The kids' schools, both single sex, were less than a mile apart from each other. Sukhdev was first to be dropped off. 'I'll pick you up after school son,' shouted Mr Singh as Sukhdev jumped out of the car and ran off to catch up with a couple of his mates, who were just going through the school gates. Suddenly he stopped, turned and ran back to the car before Mr Singh could pull out into the traffic. His tap on the car window could just be heard above the ticking of the indicator. Mr Singh rolled down the window and lowered the volume on the cassette of classical Indian music he'd just put on.

'Dad, don't bother picking me up, I can make my own way home.'

'Come on Sukh,' shouted his friends, 'we're going to be late.'

Mr Singh stared at his son for a few seconds. 'OK son.' He eased the car out into the flow of traffic.

Mr Singh dropped his daughter off and then headed for the warehouse. Outside in the car park was the usual mixture of Datsun and Mercedes cars. A caste system had operated in India for thousands of years. Only the other day he had sat down with his two children to talk about arranged marriages, and explain to them how the caste system worked. Back home in India the farmers, or Jats as they were known, were the landowners and so the top caste. Just below them in the pecking order were the Thakan, or carpenters, and below them were the Bhupia, a sort of travelling salesmen. At the bottom of the pile were the Dalit, or untouchables, who were normally unpaid farm workers, or shit-shovellers. Mr Singh explained that no one should marry below their caste, and to do so would bring shame upon their family. Even here in England the caste or class system was still carried on. But now it seemed that to some people the car you drove meant more than the caste you came from. It seemed that the respect these people gave you, and your social standing in their eyes, depended on the make of car you drove.

Mr Singh parked up and went inside. Mr Ali's warehouse was more of a male social club, with men standing around in groups chatting about business and exchanging gossip. Mr Singh nodded to a few familiar faces and shook hands with the proprietor. He grabbed a trolley, pulled a shopping list from his back pocket and headed around the aisles, which were jam-packed with boxes of food from everywhere in the world, drinks, household goods and greeting cards. The warehouse was a real Aladdin's cave. Once his trolley was loaded, Mr Singh joined the long queue at the checkout. Mr Ali and his two sons worked away at shortening the queue as quickly as they possibly could. Every time the till dinged and another sale registered, a smile would spread across their faces. It seemed money meant happiness in the Ali household. Mr Singh could see Mr Ali's wife and two daughters through the glass door of the office. They manned the phones and did all the paperwork. You never saw them out in the warehouse. Come to think of it, he had never seen any woman working or buying in Mr Ali's.

He loaded up the car and headed back home, the boot and backseat full to the brim. Two beeps of the car horn at the rear of the shop was the signal for Mr Singh's dad to raise the garage door from inside. The garage acted as an ideal storeroom. The local herberts knew this and they had had numerous break-in attempts, hence the garage door only opening from the inside. He noticed some fresh markings in the timber framework, as if someone had been attempting to saw or hack off one of the door hinges. Maybe a big dog is the answer, he began to think.

Mr Singh backed the car into the garage and unloaded his

purchases onto the shelves he'd put up. He was quite proud of his bit of DIY. There was just time for a quick cup of tea, and then he was back out in the front of the shop, serving behind the post office counter. He looked up at the clock, which said 3.45 p.m. A minute later he checked the watch on his wrist. 3.46 p.m., it read. Sukhdev should be home soon, he was thinking. He was worried; he knew he should have gone and picked the boy up. Why had he listened to his son? He didn't like to show his wife that he was unduly concerned about his son's lateness and recent run-in with the local youths, but none the less he checked his watch again as he filled in and handed over a tax disc for a customer's car. As he bent his head to place the money in the till, the sound of the bell as the shop door opened had his head popping up quicker than a jack-in-the-box.

'Hiya Dad,' said Manjit, walking into the shop. Mr Singh smiled at her and checked the time once more. It was 4.15 p.m. and there was still no sign of his son. 'Have you seen your brother?'

'No,' said Manjit. 'Why, is there a problem?'

'No, no,' her dad reassured her, looking behind him and checking the clock on the wall. 'It's just that he's not normally . . . Oh, it's just me being silly. Forget it.'

Manjit dropped her dufflebag at the bottom of the stairs that led up to the flat from the inside of the shop.

'Kids,' said Mr Singh as he moved the bag and mumbled about untidiness and somebody breaking their neck falling over it. As he picked the bag up he noticed that the back of it was covered in spots of white spit and green phlegm. Mr Singh emptied its contents onto the shop floor and, with the bag dangling from one finger, carried it outside and dumped it into a yellow rubbish bin fixed to a lamppost. As he looked up he could hear laughter. On the second floor of the tower block opposite was a line of half-a-dozen kids, heads bobbing up and spitting saliva down onto anybody who happened to be passing. They seemed to think it was highly amusing.

'Oi, you dirty, filthy animals!' yelled Mr Singh, and the spitting heads ducked down and disappeared from view.

'Leave them alone, they're only having a bit of fun,' said a man passing by on his way to the pub next door to Mr Singh's shop. Lil, the lady who ran the nearby bakers, came out of her shop to see what all the fuss and shouting was about. 'Dirty little gits,' she said. 'I've stood in my shop watching the dirty little bastards for the last half-hour. I blame the parents. They go off to work all day and leave them to fend for themselves. They don't give a damn what they get up to. It seems they couldn't care less if they went to school or not.'

Mr Singh's wife came out of the shop and stood by his side. He explained to her how he had found their daughter's bag covered in spit. She shook her head in disgust and stood there in silence, lost for words. 'Has anyone phoned the police?' she asked.

'What's the point?' said Lil. 'They'll turn up a day later and then say like they always do that if nobody is hurt, there's not a lot they can do about it.'

'Are you sure it was spit, and not a pigeon that had messed on Manjit's bag?' Mrs Singh asked her husband. He began to get annoyed.

'Well, without smelling the said substance, and without catching and taking the accused bird to the vet to check it for diarrhoea, and without going into too much graphic detail, I'd say the substance I saw on the bag was too runny and transparent to be bird shit.'

Lil let out a stifled giggle and even Mrs Singh smiled. Her

husband had a point. All the evidence pointed to the block of flats across the way.

As they turned and walked back towards the shop a police car pulled up and two uniforms got out. 'Something up?' said the driver as he placed his helmet on his head and fastened his trousers back up. No doubt his lunch had put a strain on his regulation-issue police trousers, and now the relief of letting his bulging belly have some freedom had come to a temporary end. Mr Singh explained that some kids were spitting over the balcony from the flats opposite. The policeman licked his lips and tried to remove something that was bothering him, which was hanging from the corner of his mouth. In the end he gave up and wiped his mouth with the back of his hand. A piece of the Cornish pasty he'd been stuffing his face with earlier fell from his hand and as he brushed himself down, bits of pastry and crumbs fell to the pavement. 'Now, sir, you were saying,' said the copper, as if he'd been waiting for Mr Singh to explain what was going on. Mr Singh took up the story, and said that some kids were hanging over the balcony and spitting on passers-by. He told how his daughter's bag had been covered in the stuff and how he'd thrown it in the rubbish bin. 'They are nothing but dirty animals, they're savages,' said Mr Singh angrily. At that moment a head popped up from behind the balcony wall on the third floor and looked across to where the policeman was standing.

'Look, there they are,' shouted Mr Singh, pointing upwards.

The two coppers took off and sprinted towards the main entrance of the tower block. Once through the front door, one leapt up the concrete steps and the other went for the lift. He stood there stabbing at the floor numbers on the two control panels. The metal door opened and he rushed inside. The one bounding up the stairs was shouting, 'Stop, police!' This was real

Keystone Cops stuff, for as the copper was going up in one lift, the kids were coming down in the other. Two helmeted heads poked over the third-floor balcony as half a dozen kids sauntered out and looked up, waved and laughed. Just then a bus turned up and the kids jumped on board and ran up the stairs. Off the bus stepped Sukhdev, looking a bit bewildered by what was going on. The two policemen had given up the chase by now. One tucked his white shirt back into his waistband as the other removed his helmet to wipe the sweat from his forehead. 'Fucking kids,' he mumbled under his breath.

'So, where have you been son?' asked Mr Singh as he put a protective arm around Sukhdev's shoulder, at the same time taking a crafty look at the watch on his wrist. 'Your mother was worried about you.'

'What, and you weren't?' said Sukhdev, giving his dad a quizzical look. He reminded his father that he'd told him yesterday about the hockey match that had been on that day after school. He knew his father was the one that was really the worrier. Mum was the business brain, the one with the get-up-and-go, the one that would have a bash at anything, the one who would say 'what have we got to lose'. Dad was the head of the family, and as with most Asian families the women were meant to be seen and not heard. On the whole Mum abided by these unwritten rules, but without her strength Dad would be lost.

The next day Mr Singh went out and bought Manjit a new school bag. Things began to settle down. The local kids would still try stealing from the shop, and would look out for Sukhdev to give him some grief. His uncle Teginter had given him a good tip when he'd last visited. He had told Sukhdev to carry his hockey stick with him when he came home from school. That way, said his uncle, other kids would see him carrying it and wouldn't want to pick fights, because he would have one of the longest jabs in the world. 'Use it as a weapon if need be,' said Teginter, and he was right. Overall, things began to improve. Mr Singh had even gone into the Tavern on the Green, the estate's only pub, with his brother-in-law for a drink one Saturday evening. Although they got some funny looks and a few snide comments like 'What's happened to your head?' and 'Is that your elephant in the car park?' they had quite an enjoyable evening, on the whole. The pair of them must have sunk a good few drinks while they were in there, because the next morning, besides nursing the mother of all hangovers, Mr Singh was also the proud owner of a Mercedes estate car, courtesy of his brother-in-law, who'd let him have it for what he had paid for it, or so he said. Mr Singh reminded himself never to drink whisky again. Still, a Merc would rocket him up the status ladder and get tongues wagging down at Mr Ali's.

THREE

LYNN

Lynn chewed the end of the pen she was using to fill in the loan application form she had found in an old daily newspaper she'd picked up at the doctor's surgery. She had filled in her name, address and age, but she knew in her heart that it was a waste of time. Her application would be turned down. When she came to the section of the form that said 'sex', she wrote in it 'yes please and plenty of it'.

She screwed up the form and tossed it into the wastepaper bin next to the telly. Lynn was in dire financial straits. She had no job, no money and three kids all under the age of eight. She looked down at her youngest, the product of a one-night stand with a man she had met in a local nightclub. Despite her attempts to let him know he was the father of a beautiful baby boy, who was now coming up to one year of age, she'd been unable to trace him. Lynn had even named the child Tommy, after his dad. Well, she remembered him calling himself Tom. Other than that she knew very little about him. All she could recall was that he was in his early twenties, had thick, dark, curly hair, was extremely good-looking and spoke with a soft Irish accent. He'd said he was studying engineering at a nearby university and that he missed his family and friends back home. Lynn had fallen for his charms and invited him back to her flat. Her mum was babysitting her two children, so a night of passion was on the cards.

The next morning they had shared a cup of tea and some embarrassed looks, and he had left with a kiss on her cheek, promising to come and see her that night. But he never showed, and a month or so later Lynn discovered to her horror that she was pregnant. She already had two other kids. The eldest, Ben, she'd had with her common-law husband, who had left home just after he was born saying that he couldn't cope with a kid in his life and disappeared back to West Africa, where his parents still lived. Her daughter Nancy, the middle child, was now five and had not long started school.

Lynn looked at the photograph of her three kids on the mantelpiece above the gas fire. She bent down and picked up little Tommy, pulling his bum towards her face. 'I think you need changing, young man,' she said as she laid him on the rug in front of the fire. She peeled off his dirty nappy and, holding onto him with one hand, stretched across the floor with the other and pulled the baby bag which contained Tommy's nappies and cream towards her. Tommy smiled and laughed, showing his mum the four small white teeth which had just come through and happily gurgling 'mamma' at her. Lynn tickled under his arms and kissed his belly as she secured the clean nappy. Tommy stood unsteadily and put his arms around her neck as Lynn tapped his bum and fastened the poppers on his vest.

Having finished the chore, she gave Tommy some breakfast, flicked the kettle on and searched for a clean cup. The plastic bowl in the sink was full of dirty dishes. She checked the cupboard above her head. Nothing. She'd have to wash a cup.

The kettle boiled and Lynn poured out the hot water and made herself an instant coffee. She walked back into the living-room and put the cup down on the scratched and marked coffee table, with its ring marks where previous hot cups had been placed on the varnished surface. Lynn reached over and pulled a packet of cigarettes towards her. Her chair creaked and wobbled as she sat down and looked inside it. There was one fag left. She lit it up, took a long, hard drag and blew the smoke out through her nostrils.

Relaxing for a moment, she sipped the coffee and looked around her. Three months she had lived here and she still had nothing. Lynn had watched as her new neighbours carried their belongings into the other flats from neatly loaded removal lorries. Lynn's stuff had been hurriedly packed in carrier bags and cardboard boxes and transported in the back of a friend's car. The dining-room table and chairs were a gift from her old next-door neighbours, the settee was once her mum's and the fireside rug and lampshade she had drunkenly picked up from outside a charity shop on her way home from the pub one night. Lynn had given them a good home, so, as whoever had left them intended, they had gone to a good cause. She had no carpets down and her only entertainment was a small portable black-and-white telly, which she had bought herself years ago when she had lived at home with her mum. At least the new flat had been newly decorated when she moved in, and in some rooms you could still smell the fresh paint.

Tommy rolled around the floor playing with some of his brother and sister's toys. Lynn stubbed out the dog end of her cigarette and put the empty cup back in the bowl with the rest of the washing up. Her letter-box rattled, and onto the plastic tiled floor fell some post. Lynn bent down and picked it up. She began to talk out aloud to herself. 'Gas bill, electric bill, rent.' She shoved all of the envelopes, unopened, into one of the bulging kitchen drawers along with the rest of the bills and final demands. It was time to get Ben and Nancy up for school. She went into the bedroom they shared and pulled back the curtains. The shaft of bright sunlight shining in made them stir immediately in their bunk beds.

'Good morning precious Prince and Princess.' She gently pulled back the covers on each of their beds as they stretched and yawned. 'Come on, sweethearts, chop chop, rise and shine. It's time to get up for school.' The two of them slowly came round and lowered themselves out of bed and onto the cold floor. They followed their mum down the stairs. Little Tommy's face lit up when he saw his brother and sister. Lynn made them a bowl of porridge each and a beaker of orange squash. Tommy was still sucking and munching on the last of his Marmite on bread soldiers.

Once the kids had finished they were dressed and ready for school. Lynn strapped Tommy in his buggy and off they went. It was only a brisk ten-minutes on foot to their school, with Ben and Nancy walking along at a brisk pace next to the pram. On the way Lynn stopped at Mr Singh's shop and picked up a packet of crisps each for the two eldest kids. She also got a packet of custard cream biscuits, which she would break in half and put in the kid's lunchboxes. This was to be their midday meal. At the moment she couldn't afford school dinners and had applied for free meals. She had filled in numerous forms and spoken to the headmistress, but had heard nothing. Until such time as she did, the kids would have to get by on what she could rustle up. Some days, if there were bread in the house and something to put in it, she would make them up a sandwich, but on the days when the cupboard was bare they would have to make do. Mr Singh wrote the items Lynn had chosen down in his red book. Lynn bought things on tick at Mr Singh's with the promise that she would settle up at the end of the week, but she never did. It wasn't that she didn't want to, she just never seemed to have any money left come the end of the week. She was behind with the rent and was deeply in debt. The money she got from the social just didn't seem to go anywhere.

Mr Singh reminded her that her bill now stood at nearly £80. 'Lynn, I'm afraid you are going to have to pay what you owe before I can let you have anything else on tick,' he said as he took her shopping from her and put it to one side.

'Come on Mr Singh,' said Lynn, almost pleading, 'just the kid's food and some nappies and twenty fags, and I'll come in tonight or tomorrow and settle up with you.' Mr Singh raised his eyebrows and turned to his wife, who was stacking the shelves. He spoke to her in Punjabi. 'OK,' he said, 'but Mrs Singh says this is the last credit you get.'

Lynn smiled and thanked Mr and Mrs Singh as she slipped the shopping into the plastic carrier bag hanging from the handles of the buggy. 'I'll be in as soon as I've cashed my cheque and I'll clear the debt,' she said as she wheeled the buggy from the shop.

They headed in the direction of the school, which was situated on the edge of the estate. On the way they caught up with Sharon, another single mum who lived a couple of floors up from Lynn. Ben and Sharon's daughter were in the same class at school. As the children ran along together Lynn and Sharon chatted away.

'I'm glad I bumped into you,' said Sharon. 'What are you doing tonight?'

'Why?' asked Lynn.

'The Tavern on the Green's football team are having a disco.'

'I'd love to come,' said Lynn, 'and thanks for thinking of me, but I'm skint and I can't possibly afford to go out.'

'Look' said Sharon, 'it'll be my treat, I'm flush for a few quid.

THE ESTATE

My estranged husband asked me to look after some money for him the other week. He said he'd done a building job for a fella who'd paid him in cash. More like he'd robbed some poor old fucker. Anyway, I agreed to look after it for him and he even bunged me a couple of hundred quid on top, so that me and the little ones can treat ourselves. He ended up getting arrested and last week the dickhead got eighteen months' bird for deception. So I reckon he won't be needing the money for a while. Anyway, it would only be like me deducting my bank charges.' Lynn and Sharon both laughed.

'Well,' said Lynn, 'it sounds very tempting. I could do with a night out. Staring at the same four walls every night drives me potty.'

'I'll take that as a yes then,' said Sharon.

'Yeah, go on then,' replied Lynn. She kissed the kids goodbye at the school gates and wheeled little Tommy back round to his nan's house.

Lynn's mum suffered from arthritis and lived in a small bungalow on the estate. Lynn relied on her a lot, not just financially, but also as a shoulder to cry on and someone to sit and have a moan with. Lynn picked Tommy up from the buggy and lifted her mum's letterbox.

'Nana!' the baby shouted, rattling the metal flap. Tommy screeched with excitement as he saw his nan coming down the passageway.

'Coming darling,' said Nan, smiling as she saw a pair of big brown eyes looking through the slit in the door. She opened her front door and smothered the little fella in kisses, and pinched his cheeks as she wiped the bright red lipstick from his chubby chops.

'I'll put the kettle on,' Nan said as they followed her down the hallway and into the kitchen. The first thing she did was to put the clear plastic biscuit box down on the carpet and let

Tommy bury his arm up to his elbow as he sorted out his favourite chocolate ones.

'Mum, any chance of a favour tonight?' Lynn asked.

'Lynn, if it's money you're wanting, you've no chance. I'm skint.'

Lynn shook her head and explained that Sharon had asked her to go out and would be paying, and that she was just wondering if her mum would help her out by babysitting. Lynn's mum was like putty in her hands when it came to the three kids, and it took all of two seconds for her to agree that she would have them.

'Mum, you're a star.' Lynn jumped up and hugged her. 'I'll bring them over to you straight from school. That way they can have some tea with their nan, and you can give them a bath and read them a story before you get them ready for bed.' Lynn smiled at her mum.

Later that day she left Tommy with his nan while she picked up the other two from school and dropped them off. Before she left to go home and get ready, her mum had a quiet word with her as they sat at the kitchen table. 'Go steady tonight love,' she said. Lynn looked at her, knowing what she meant. 'Be careful, that's all I'm saying. Don't have too much to drink and make a fool of yourself.' Lynn knew full well what she was getting at. She wanted Lynn to learn to say no, to take some pride in herself and not jump into bed with the first man to take an interest in her. 'I think I know what you mean,' said Lynn, embarrassed at her mum's allusion to her past behaviour. 'I know my track record with men hasn't been exactly good,' she agreed, 'but I'm a big girl now and I'm old enough to be able to go out on my own without you worrying.' Nan stood up and started to prepare the kids' tea. 'Lynn, all I'm saying is you've already got three kids and neither you nor I want any more.' This was something that cropped up every time Lynn and her mum had words. Lynn kissed the children and told them Mummy would see them in the morning.

'Cheers Mum. I don't know what I'd do without you,' she smiled.

'Go on,' said Nan. 'Go out and have a good time.' She pulled Lynn towards her and they hugged and kissed one another on the cheek. Three small faces looked around the kitchen door, smiling and giggling. Lynn and her mum both laughed and bent down to kiss the kids again.

Back home Lynn poured herself a glass of red wine, the last of a bottle she'd opened the night before. She smoked a cigarette as she stepped into the hot bath water and flicked the half-finished fag out of the bathroom window. She was excited about going out that night. It was ages since she had been out for a night on the town, but what her mum had said was still swirling around in her head. She lay back and began to drift off, thinking of Tom, her one-night lover. She could almost feel him kissing her softly on the lips, darting his tongue in and out of her mouth. In her daydream he nibbled her ears and kissed down both sides of her neck, working slowly down her body and caressing her all over until his hand reached between her legs, stroking the inside of her thighs. Her heart began to pound, and her hand became Tom's hand as she touched herself gently. Her body felt like it was about to explode. 'Oh Tom, that's beautiful,' she murmured. 'Please don't leave me this time.'

'You little fuckers, leave things fucking alone!' Lynn slid bolt upright in her bath, sending water over the sides. Her daydream had been interrupted by her neighbour, shouting and screaming at her kids. The peaceful silence was broken. The trouble was you could hear a pin drop through these paper-thin walls.

Lynn wrapped a towel around herself and sat on the edge of her bed to light up another fag. That dream had brought back some happy yet painful memories and she stared into space for a while without moving. She had not had peace and quiet like this for years. No screaming or crying kids. No shouts of 'Mum, can I have a drink? Mum, what's for dinner? Mum, can we have some sweets?' She lay back on the bed and drifted off to sleep.

It was a couple of hours before Lynn came round and she felt so much better. She did her hair and make up, and picked out some nice matching underwear to put on under the skimpy black strapless dress she planned on wearing. Although she didn't go to a gym or do any regular exercise, and despite having three children, Lynn had always managed to keep her trim figure, a figure most teenagers would be proud of. She scrubbed up well, she told herself, and when she was all dolled up she looked a million dollars and could turn most men's heads.

She slipped on her little black number, put the finishing touches to her long blonde hair and checked herself in the bathroom mirror, turning this way and that. She was happy with how she looked.

The doorbell went and she slipped on her high-heeled shoes before walking along the passageway to open the door. Standing there done up to the nines was Sharon, her red, tight-fitting dress struggling to contain her chest. 'You ready then darling?' she asked.

'Let me get me coat and I'll be right with you.'

Lynn slammed the front door shut behind her and the pair of them clip-clopped along the balcony in their high heels. A couple of teenagers having a fag and kicking a football on the landing outside the lifts looked over and giggled. One of them came out with something about mutton dressed up as lamb.

'Mutton dressed up as pig more like it,' said his friend.

'Cheeky little bastards,' laughed the girls. They chatted away nervously about the night ahead as they went down in the lift.

THE ESTATE

It was a short walk out of the front entrance of the flats across the playing field and past the community centre and shops to the pub. A car full of blokes passed and they sounded the horn and shouted at the girls.

'Fuck off and get some hair around your bollocks, you silly little kids!' shouted Sharon as she gave them a two-fingered salute.

They carried on walking. Suddenly a car pulled up alongside them. It was Terry, the cabbie. 'Hop in girls, I'll give you a lift.'

'No, it's all right Tel, we're only going over to the Tavern.'

'I might just see you there later' said Terry, flashing his yellow-stained teeth as he smiled.

'That fucking bloke gives me the bleedin' creeps,' Lynn shivered.

'It was nice of him to stop and offer us a lift though.'

'Mm,' said Lynn, still not sure about him.

They passed Mr Singh, sweeping up outside his shop. He was speaking to Justin, who owned the hairdressers next door to the Singhs, and was asking him about dogs.

'You've got a guard dog, haven't you?'

'It's hardly that,' said Justin. 'I somehow don't think Yorkshire Terriers are classed as guard dogs.'

Mr Singh looked none the wiser; this dog business was confusing. Luckily he had his back to Lynn as they passed. Mr Singh would have to wait for his money.

Outside the pub they stopped and took a breath. 'Here goes,' said Sharon as they pulled at the saloon bar door and stepped inside. It was smoky and the music loud as they tried to adjust their eyes to the darkness. The disco lights flashed and it seemed that dozens of pairs of eyes were on them. They found a gap at the bar and ordered two large vodka and tonics and looked round for somewhere to sit. The only available table was next to the men's toilets, so they plonked themselves down and carried on chatting. Although they knew one another, it was

34

mainly in passing. They normally only spoke outside the school gates as they dropped the kids off or picked them up. Tonight was a good chance to find out more about each other and have a bit of a chinwag. It turned out that Sharon's older sister had been in the same class as Lynn at secondary school and that her auntie had lived next door to Lynn's uncle at one time.

The girls glanced around and noticed a group of blokes looking over at them. It seemed they were geeing one another up to see who would be first to go over and chat them up. Two blokes broke away from the group and sauntered over. 'Evening girls' said one of them, staring at the girls' chests. They smiled as the blokes pulled up chairs and put their pints on the table. 'Would you like a drink ladies?'

'Yes please,' said Sharon, 'we'd both like a large vodka and tonic.'

'Go on, get the girls a drink,' said the one who had spoken to his mate.

'I'll give you a hand,' said Sharon tugging down her dress and checking that her tits were still where they were meant to be. Lynn sat where she was and smiled at the man opposite. Above the sound of the music she could just make out that he was telling her his name was Steve. 'I'm the captain of the pub football team. This year we won the championship and I got voted the club's player of the year.'

Lynn smiled as Sharon came back from the bar and put the drinks on the table. She winked at Lynn. 'All right sweetheart?'

'Yeah, she's fine,' said Steve as he shifted his chair next to Lynn's and put his arm around her. 'I'll look after her.' The barmaid stared over, through the crowded bar, giving Lynn a dirty look and making her feel uneasy. 'What's her problem?' she asked.

'That's Kerry, the landlord's daughter, I used to go out with her. You know how ex-girlfriends can be. I think she still has a crush on me,' said Steve, staring back at her behind the bar.

'More drinks anyone?' asked Steve's pal, as Steve handed some money over for the next round of drinks.

'I'll come with you,' said Sharon. 'Looks like Lynn's sorted here.'

Steve and Lynn tried to have a conversation above the sound of the pounding music and after a couple more rounds of drinks, Lynn's head was spinning and she felt quite drunk and lightheaded. She looked around for Sharon, who seemed to have disappeared. Steve suggested they go outside for some fresh air. She agreed, but was a little unsteady on her feet as she stood up and wobbled her way through the crowded bar. Someone in the crowd grabbed her and pinched her arse, but she ignored it and kept going. As she went she heard a wolf whistle and noticed some blokes slapping Steve on the back. 'Get in there, son,' she heard a voice say.

Outside it was dark and she leant back onto the wall of the pub. Steve wasted no time at all as he kissed her and pushed himself against her. 'Come on darling,' he said. 'We're both adults. You know what I want, so let's go back to your place or mine.' He leaned forward to kiss her. Lynn turned her head away. He grabbed her tits with both hands and she pushed him away in disgust.

'You fucking prickteaser,' he snarled. Lynn picked up her bag and slipped on her coat, which was around her shoulders, and walked off. Kerry the barmaid had followed them out. 'Steve, what's going on?' she asked.

'Nothing,' he replied. 'Just her getting a bit fresh and coming on to me.'

'You fucking old dog!' he suddenly shouted in a temper.

Lynn stopped and turned around to face him. 'Well, tonight my mum would be proud of me. Goodnight.'

FOUR

JUSTIN AND TONY

Justin swept the last of the hair on the salon floor into a neat pile. He leant the broom up against the wall and checked his own hair in the mirror, fiddled with the collar on his shirt and then bent down with a dustpan and brush and with one single swoop swept the hair up and tipped it into the bin. 'Tony darling,' he said in his best camp voice, 'would you care to join me for a quick drink?' Justin put his broom away in the store cupboard and turned the sign on the front door from 'Open' to 'Closed'. Tony finished washing his hands in the white porcelain sink and took the glass of chilled white wine Justin had poured for him. He took a sip and slumped into one of the red leather hairdressing chairs. Justin sat next to him and swivelled round on his chair. Round and round he went, like a kid on his favourite fairground ride.

'Will you please keep still and stop fucking about,' said Tony sternly.

Justin stopped, leant over and gave Tony a kiss full on the lips. 'Sweetheart, shall we have an early night?' he asked.

Tony didn't answer, but instead stood up and started to

clean the mirrors and tidy the shelves and work surfaces. Shampoo went on one, conditioner on another, brushes and combs in one drawer, towels in the other. Justin looked at him. 'Is something bothering you? Have I upset you?'

Tony stared back at Justin and his face broke out into a smile. 'No, it's nothing. It's just me being a prat.'

'Thank fuck for that. I thought I had done something seriously wrong, or that you were about to tell me you'd found someone else.'

Tony laughed. Justin was so insecure. They had been together for over eight years, and for seven of those they had lived and worked together in their own salon. In the beginning it was Justin's business and Tony had started working in the shop as a 16-year-old Saturday boy. Justin had taken him under his wing. He was a big, strapping lad who liked football and rugby and was a bit of a lady's man. He didn't look the type who'd want to be a hairdresser. In fact, he'd wanted to join the army when he left school and do an apprenticeship with the Royal Corp. of Transport, even going so far as to pass the required exam and medical, but at the last minute he had bottled out. That was after Justin had taken him out for a farewell meal and poured his heart out to him. He had finally admitted his feelings for Tony. A couple of bottles of wine later and the pair were in bed at Justin's flat.

Tony kept his sexuality from his mum and dad for years. Although they suspected that something was going on, Tony kept up the pretence that his and Justin's relationship was purely platonic and that they were just business partners. Then, one day, after a row with his father, Tony came clean and admitted that he and Justin were lovers. His mum cried tears of joy, threw her arms around him and said she was happy for them both. His dad on the other hand, was devastated and found it very hard to accept. He came out with the usual bullshit; why in all the world did he have to have a son that was a raving poof? Then he stormed out of the house and went to do some work on his allotment. He stayed there until the early hours of the morning and returned red-eyed. When Tony's mum asked if he had been crying, he had replied, 'Don't be so daft woman, I've been handling spring onions.'

Justin's mum had always known he was gay. She said that even before he went to his first school, he loved to dress up in his big sister Emily's frocks and play with her dolls and toy pram. He would spend hours brushing and plaiting his own and his sister's hair – he'd rather do that than play football with the other boys out on the street. His mum had just accepted the way her son was and so did all her friends, relatives and neighbours. Everyone knew Justin was gay, so why should she give a shit? He was her son and she loved him so that was that. Her new bloke had never met Justin, but he was sure to have heard plenty about him. Justin's dad had died at an early age, from cancer. Justin was only ten when he lost his dad so suddenly and he missed him terribly. His mum had brought him and Emily up as best she could. At one time she was doing three jobs a day to try to make ends meet, but the kids never went without.

Justin and his mum being particularly close, there was nothing he wouldn't tell her. She was his best friend. They'd hang out together and she would often give him her opinion on his latest boyfriend. She had been a bit of a girl in her time, and before she was married she'd been an art student and had travelled extensively. She'd spent a couple of years in India and had worked for a year on a kibbutz in Israel. She spoke many languages fluently and looked far younger than her 60 years – she could quite easily pass for someone in their early 40s.

THE ESTATE

Tony was touchy that day because his parents were coming over to dinner the next day, along with Justin's mum and her new man friend, and a couple of Tony and Justin's friends. 'So what's bothering you about the dinner party?' Justin asked Tony, concerned that he might go deeper into one of his long drawn-out moods. Tony didn't answer, but sat looking in the mirror and fiddling with his hair and bushy moustache. Then he got up and slipped on his jacket. 'Come on,' he said, 'let's go down the local for a couple of pints.' Justin slipped the lead on Rocky their pet Yorkie and off they went.

'It's not very lively in here for a Saturday night,' said Tony looking around the nearly empty pub. The few people that were in there gave the two of them the usual stares and made snide remarks. A couple of the football team came in and plonked their kit bags down on the floor next to the bar. They looked over in Tony and Justin's direction. 'I see the shirtlifters are in then,' said one. 'No one bend over in front of them,' said another. Tony and Justin ignored them and just carried on talking. Most people on the estate accepted and liked the couple. The blue-rinse brigade and all the women and teenagers who came in to the salon to have their hair done got on well with them. Their customers enjoyed coming in for a chat and have a coffee. They had no problem. Some of the fellas, though, were less than friendly, and the two of them were seen as something of a threat by a few. Although there had been no direct challenges, it seemed that gay and straight young men from around these parts would definitely not be seen arm-in-arm.

They drank up and as they went to leave one of the football players wolf-whistled 'See ya ducky!' he shouted. Tony turned and walked towards the bar where the voice had come from. Standing there with his mate, both of them with smirks on their faces, was Steve, the captain of the football team. Tony pushed his face half-an-inch from Steve's pock-marked red nose and stood on the lout's foot as he spoke to him. He did think about showing him up in front of his mates by kissing him full on the lips, but he was put off by the smell of his breath.

'Got a problem big mouth?'

Steve's bottom lip began to tremble and he could feel his face going a deep shade of red. His ears began to burn and his eyes filled with tears.

'Have you got a problem?' Tony asked again.

'Tony, leave it, please,' said Justin. 'Let's just go home.'

'Well, answer me.'

Steve wouldn't even look Tony in the eye. He hung his head and stared at the pattern of fag burns on the carpet. He fidgeted nervously as his now not-so-mouthy friend looked the other way and pretended he wasn't part of this.

Even Dave the landlord said nothing as he stood on the other side of the bar drying glasses with a cloth. He for one didn't care for Steve. He had once found his wife in a passionate embrace with him in the back garden at a friend's party. On seeing this Dave had stormed off, but his wife had gone after him and explained that she'd had too much to drink and hadn't been able to find him to tell him she didn't feel too good. She had gone outside by herself to get some fresh air. Steve must have followed her out. Next thing she knew he had grabbed hold of her and tried to kiss her. She'd pushed him off and tried to get away, and that's when Dave had come out. Dave wanted to go back and punch his lights out, but Wendy had persuaded him not to, persuading him that it would all be sorted out when everyone was sober. Steve had also been going out with Dave's step-daughter Kerry on and off for the past year and had messed her about, asking her to get engaged, and to go on holiday with him to Spain, then saying that he needed time on his own to think things through. In fact, he was more disliked than anybody else on the estate. He was nothing but a loud-mouthed bully who was at last getting what he deserved.

The rest of the football team came in and stood frozen, staring in disbelief at what they were seeing.

'Come on mate, let him go,' said Steve's mate, suddenly finding his voice. 'He hasn't done anything wrong. He was only having a laugh.'

Tony smiled. 'Perhaps Mr Hard-nut here should stick to picking on girls like he did with a certain young lady the other night.' Tony pulled a five-pound note from his trouser pocket and threw it onto the polished counter. 'Here Dave, get these two girls a Babycham each.' He turned and left, leaving everyone laughing at Steve the bully and his not-so-brave mate.

The doorbell rang and Justin and Tony both jumped to their feet. Rocky ran to the front door, barking and wagging his tail at the same time. The two men knew without having to speak what the other had to do. Justin went along the passage to get the front door, whilst Tony turned the television off and checked how dinner was doing in the oven. Not that he had a clue how to tell – Justin was the chef. He had just ducked into the kitchen to get out of the way. He was really quite a shy person and liked Justin to do all the welcoming and 'pleased to see you' bit.

Justin's voice was just audible talking to someone at the door and, by the sounds of it, their first guests had arrived. He got glasses down from the cupboard and poured out some wine. 'Tony, your mum and dad are here,' Justin called out, with not a hint of campness in his suddenly acquired deep voice. Tony came out and greeted his parents. He kissed his mum, but was never sure how to welcome his dad. Did he kiss him? Dad decided for him, holding out his hand.

'Wine Mum, wine Dad?'

'Please, son,' they both answered.

The two couples sat down and the silence was deafening as they all looked at one another. Tony's mum broke the ice. 'How's the business doing?'

'Yeah, great,' Justin replied. The doorbell rang and Justin stood up, glad of the excuse to get out of the room for a moment. Tony's dad made it so obvious that he didn't like his son being in a gay relationship. He was embarrassed that the two of them were living together like a married couple. Justin's mum and her boyfriend Ron came in and while the two sets of parents were being introduced Justin went to the kitchen to keep an eye on how the dinner was doing. His mum followed and gave her son a huge hug and a wet kiss. Justin wiped his mouth with the back of his hand and looked at the smears of rose-red lipstick that had come off his mum's lips. Lots of women of his mother's age tended to wear that colour, he thought. It was a sort of '40s film star look.

Justin prodded the potatoes to see if they were done, then opened the oven and turned over the pieces of salmon which were cooking in there. A delicious smell of olive oil, garlic and herbs filled the kitchen. Out came the prawn cocktail starters from the fridge, along with a big bowl of freshly prepared salad for the centre of the table. Justin put some garlic bread wrapped in silver foil into the oven. 'I reckon there's enough for everyone, don't you Ma?' His mum smiled. She remembered Justin as a young lad helping her out in the kitchen, making cakes and gingerbread men. He had been very creative and artistic from a young age, and she'd always thought he would one day make his living as a chef.

Justin's mum looked through the serving-hatch into the dining-room to make sure everyone was getting along OK. Her boyfriend Ron could talk for England. He never stopped. Tony and his mum were laughing and joking as he kept them all entertained, but Tony's dad sat there stone-faced, hardly saying a word. He was making it plainly obvious that he wasn't happy about being there. Tony made sure everyone's glasses were topped up and changed the music on the stereo, then escaped into the kitchen to check if the food was nearly ready and that Justin and his mum were all right.

'Your dad looks happy,' said Justin sarcastically, peering through the serving hatch. 'Yeah,' said Tony. 'He's not the happiest man in the world.' Justin's mum busied herself around the kitchen and carried the starters through to the dinner table, which with all credit to the boys was beautifully set. They had laid out their best silver cutlery and good dinner service, and a bottle of the best champagne was on ice in a silver bucket in the middle of Liberace's piano. Justin put the finishing touches to the main course, stuck a home-made apple pie in the oven and joined the others at the table.

The doorbell went again. It was Rose and Bella, the last of the guests. They came in dolled up to the nines as usual and said hello to everyone. Tony's dad looked at them, trying to work out if they were men or women. In fact they were two drag artists who had been friends of Justin's for years. 'Hello sweetheart, you've got a cheeky face,' Rose said to Tony's dad, who didn't realise he was taking the piss out of his stuffy, stern appearance. As soon as Rose said it, he went bright red and tried to avoid any more eye contact.

'I'm going in for my operation soon,' said Bella, the more effeminate of the two, who tonight for a change didn't have a dress on and was wearing conservative jeans and a checked shirt.

'Are you dear?' said Justin. Tony's dad tutted.

'Yes, I'm having the chop, so from now on I'll be the perfect woman.'

'Perfect bitch more like,' said Rose.

'Now, now,' said Justin's mum, ' no fighting please, girls.'

Tony's dad looked disgusted and suddenly blurted out, 'One day the good Lord above will extract revenge on all those that have ignored his thoughts on men sleeping with men. It's not natural and it says so in the Bible. Man, read the scriptures. It says clearly that man shall not lie with man. One day he shall release his vengeance and destroy all those that refused to listen.'

'And how, pray tell, is he going to do that, Dad?' asked Tony. 'With a plague of locusts?' Everyone around the table laughed.

'It's no good you lot laughing, because believe me, one day the Lord Jesus Christ will rid the earth of your kind and its unnatural ways. Whether by a disease that wipes you all out or by a flood or some other disaster, believe me your days are numbered.'

'You'd better phone Noah to see if he's still got that ark,' laughed Justin's mum.

'You have been warned.'

Ignoring him, Tony took out the champagne he'd had chilling in an ice bucket. 'Champers anyone?' He used a tea towel to carefully remove the cork from the neck of the bottle. As a kid he had seen a waiter in a restaurant get a cork straight in the eye after struggling to get it out of the neck of the bottle. The waiter had collapsed in agony and the bottle had slipped from his hands and smashed as he screamed in pain and fell in a heap. Blood had pumped from a gaping hole just above his eyelid. That incident had stuck with him, and he was always careful when pulling corks. He poured everyone a glass of bubbly and they all tucked into their starters. Next up was the main course, which was washed down with more chilled bubbly, and then came the apple pie, laced with brandy and served with fresh cream and finally the cheese and biscuits.

Afterwards they settled down with Justin's speciality, Irish coffees, which were so strong they made those who were not used to them wince. Then there was more wine, followed by brandy liqueurs, which loosened everyone's tongues. Ron and Justin's mum had everyone laughing with tales of their runs out to the countryside on Ron's Harley Davidson. Even Tony's dad lightened up and smiled as Ron told the tale of how they'd gone for a picnic in the countryside and halfway through their lunch had got a bit amorous. They had failed to notice a coachful of blokes out on a beano who had stopped for a piss and were now watching them over the top of a hedge.

'I didn't know where to put my face,' said Justin's mum.

'Or your tits and arse!' laughed Ron.

Justin topped everyone's glasses up, smiled at Tony and slipped his hand inside his. They looked at one another as they grasped on to each other tightly. Justin began to speak.

'Ladies and Gentlemen, Mums and Dads, I'd just like to take this opportunity whilst we're all here to say a few words. As you know, Tony and myself have been together a long time and people have described us as almost the perfect couple. If we were man and wife we would have a long and happy marriage. We work together, live together and get along together. We are so much in love.' Tony squeezed his partner's hand as Justin's voice trembled with emotion. 'I'm extremely lucky to have a partner like Tony. He's my rock, my island in a stormy sea. He is my ideal man.'

Tony's dad fiddled with his serviette and looked at his wife. She was three-parts pissed and for once couldn't care less how he felt; she was enjoying herself.

Justin continued, 'We've been an item now for almost eight

years and after talking it through, we have decided we would like to make our love complete by adopting a baby.' Ron cheered. Rose and Bella clapped and hugged, Justin's mum kissed them both and burst into tears. Tony's mum smiled and cheered as his dad almost choked on his drink. He coughed and spluttered as the champagne ran down his nostrils and he spat the rest into his napkin. 'I don't fucking believe it!' he snapped as he stood up and pushed the chair away from him with the back of his knees. He dabbed at the wet patches on his shirt and tie and threw down the napkin, screwed into a ball, on the table. 'Come on woman, we're going home.'

Tony's mum didn't move. She looked up at her husband. 'I'm going nowhere. I'm celebrating!' Everyone cheered.

'You're fucking sick, the lot of you.' He grabbed his jacket and stormed off, slamming the front door behind him.

'Another drink anyone?' giggled Tony's mum, leaning across the table to grab an unopened bottle.

FIVE

TERRY THE CABBIE

Terry drove his car slowly into the car park behind the tower block where he lived. It was 4.30 a.m. and he had just finished a twelve-hour shift in his minicab. He turned off the radio and lights and stuffed his money into a small leather purse where he kept his change. He looked around to check no one was watching and stuffed it inside his jacket pocket. He looked around again, he got out and locked the car up before disappearing into the flats. Even at this time of the morning, you had to be aware that anyone could be lurking in the shadows. Thieves didn't work nine till five. Working with the general public and driving for a living had sharpened his senses to what was going on around him.

He pressed the lift button and waited, all the time listening and looking around. He lived on the 12th floor, where he had a one-bedroom bachelor pad. The lift came down and out stepped Ernie Jones. He was a train driver who started early most mornings. Terry knew him and his wife Flo really well. They were a nice old couple that lived in the flat immediately below him. Ernie had his own allotment and whenever he brought any veg home he would knock on Terry's door and give him a bag of potatoes or carrots or runner beans or whatever was in season – in fact it seemed Ernie kept the whole block supplied with fresh veg. While Terry was out working in his cab on a couple of occasions, he had seen Ernie and his wife waiting at the bus stop in town loaded up with shopping, so he stopped and gave them a lift home and he wouldn't take a penny for it, despite their protests.

'Morning Tel.'

'Morning Ernie.' Terry climbed into the lift and pressed the button to take him up. He lent back against the shiny metal plate wall and the smell of stale piss assaulted his nostrils. Fish and chip wrappers and dog ends lay strewn over the floor. 'Fucking dirty cunts,' he said as he tip-toed his way out of the lift when he reached the top floor. He held his hand to his mouth as he stepped over a fresh pile of sick someone by the looks of it had not long honked up. His flat was right next to the lobby where the lifts were, so he only had a short walk. Just before he put the key in his front door he looked out across the estate. It was still dark and the only light came from the lamp-posts down below and the lights dotted along each balcony. It was a quiet, almost peaceful time of the day but in another three or four hours the sound of alarm clocks going off, cars starting, kids screaming and shouting, doors slamming and lifts going up and down on noisy creaky cables, would be sure to disturb his much needed sleep.

Once inside the flat, he turned on the lights, and bent down to pick up some junk mail lying on the mat. A quick glance at it and it went straight in the bin. Terry flicked the kettle on and stuck some bread under the grill. He opened the fridge and took out some milk. It didn't look too healthy so he held it up to the light and had a look. It was a bit like a yoghurt with thick grey lumps floating in it. He took the silver foil lid off and smelt it – yeah, it was off, alright. He checked the date and it was nearly a month since he had purchased it. How time flies past, he thought. I'll just have to make do with a black coffee, and he poured the hot water into a mug and buttered some toast. He flicked on the TV and flopped down onto the settee. A black-and-white war film was on one side, but he wasn't paying that much attention to it.

The last job on the shift he had just finished involved picking up a nurse from her lodgings and taking her to the hospital where she worked. It was a regular account job and over the last few months he had picked her up a few times. She was blonde, slim and very, very attractive.

They had often chatted and had a bit of a laugh together, and in a roundabout way he'd sort of asked her out. Today when she'd got in the cab her blue nurse's dress had risen up and shown off the tops of her legs and her black stockings and suspenders. Another time in the car she had lent forward to open the door to get out and her top buttons had come undone and he caught a glimpse of her black lacy bra and her ample cleavage. Sometimes when he'd dropped her off he would often sit and watch her wiggle her way into work, her lovely tight arse moving from side to side. He would daydream and imagine himself exploring her body before pulling her knickers down and doing her from behind, he'd pump away doggy style whilst wrapping his hands around her lovely shaped tits. He'd have visions of banging away for ages, unable to come as she groaned for more.

'Don't stop, don't stop,' she would scream in ecstasy.

He put his coffee cup down on the carpet and bunged the last piece of toast into his mouth as he laid back onto the settee and undid his shirt to the waist. He unzipped his trousers and lifted his stiff cock out of his white frayed jockey pants. The smell that rose up made even him puff his cheeks out, the whiff of sweat and body-odour came up as he began banging away with his right hand. He lifted his arse up and with his other hand undid his belt and slid his trousers and pants down to his knees. Now he could really go to town thinking about her. He rubbed and rubbed and groaned as he imagined pumping up and down on his randy nurse. He went through the whole scenario in his mind and he could see it like it was a TV screen. He was laying there as she stood up, and stripped down to her bra and knickers, her tits bursting from the sides and front of her bra, her black knickers revealing dark pubic hair hanging from the sides, the bulge on her crotch like the bonnet of a Volkswagen Beetle. He pulls her towards him and removes her bra, her bust rubbing in his face as he works his way down her body, his tongue darting in and out of her belly button, clearing away any unwanted fluff. He pulls her knickers to one side and begins to tongue her sweet-smelling wet pussy. He'd turn her over and give her a good . . . oh – oh, fuck, his dick was pumping out white sticky muck and it had gone all over his hands and was running in between his fingers. He'd come his lot before he'd even had time to fuck her. Next time to fulfil all his fantasies he would have to slow down when wanking. He laid back and worked his trousers and pants down to his ankles he kicked them off and lifted his legs up towards his chest and pulled off one of his socks. He wiped the spunk off his fingers onto the sock, then he lifted his dick up and gave that a wipe around. He rubbed his balls and threw the sock down onto the floor with the rest of his clothes. He rubbed his balls, smelt his fingers and closed his eyes.

Later that morning Terry was woken by the morning paper coming through his letterbox. He stretched his arms and legs and threw off the coat he had laying over him – he must have got cold in the night and got up and taken it from behind the front door where he had hung it when he came in. But then if he had walked that far, why hadn't he just gone to bed? He stood up and scratched his balls and couldn't resist smelling his fingers again. He couldn't remember the last time his prized possessions had had a soak in the bath or a shower or had even had a wet flannel and soap rubbed around them. One thing was for sure, they fucking stank. He buttoned up the creased and crumpled shirt he'd slept in and slipped on the odd sock lying on the pile of clothes next to him. He pulled the trousers from the jumble on the floor and pulled them up over his bulging belly. He wandered into the bathroom and had a piss while looking in the mirror at himself. He smiled and his stained yellow and chipped teeth looked back at him. They were the type that hadn't seen a toothbrush or toothpaste for months. He wiped some shaving foam around his jaw and gave himself a shave with a semi-blunt razor. As he shaved the metal cut both bristle and skin. He splashed some water over his face and dabbed at the blood, which was trickling down his cheek. 'Fucking poxy razor,' he moaned as he pulled a sheet of toilet paper from the roll and ripped off a tiny piece about half an inch square and stuck it over the cut. He splashed some cheap aftershave onto his face, picked the newspaper up from the mat and turned on the telly. A pretty young actress from one of the soap-powder adverts bent over showing plenty of shapely leg in a short mini-skirt, filling her washing machine up. She shows off her cleavage in a skimpy top as she wiggles and giggles her way through her two-minute slot 'I'd fucking give that one,' Terry said out aloud, as if he were talking to someone else with him in the room. He went to make himself a bowl of cereal.

THE ESTATE

'Bollocks, there's no fucking milk,' he said as he put the bowl back.

He opened up the paper for a quick check of yesterday's horseracing results. No – fuck all. Another day without his gee-gees coming in meant he had to be back out grafting in the cab. No big win and doing his dough meant another day behind the wheel. He lived in the hope that one day his accumulator or Yankee would come in and a big pay day would change his life. Maybe with his new-found fortune he'd buy a new car, go on a round-the-world cruise. Just imagine all them Yankee birds on board – all those unmarried rich old girls gagging for a night of high voltage sex. I wouldn't need their money, he thought. I'd have me own, or maybe I'd jet off to the Med and have a couple of weeks in the sun in Majorca or Ibiza – all them bikini-clad babes laying on the beach, some of them sunbathing topless . . . Just the mere thought of it caused a stir in his trousers, but then again it didn't take a lot to get Terry horny. He'd read in one of those women's magazines that men think of sex once every 15 minutes. That wasn't true in his case – he thought of sex every minute of every day, it was constantly on his mind. But the funny thing was that when he was in a relationship (and the last one was about five years ago which lasted all of two weeks) he wasn't that bothered about sex. He had been out with other women on dates but nothing serious. He had even paid for sex but that had turned out to be a disaster; he'd picked up a girl one night in a red-light area and drove off with her in his car after they'd first agreed a fee for her services. Unbeknown to him though, he was being watched by an unmarked police car which followed him down a dark lane where the prostitute had directed him. He'd just unzipped his flies when there was a tap on the window. He nearly jumped out of his skin when he saw the copper standing there. He was asked to step from the car

54

and explain what he was doing. He first told the copper that he and his fiancée were just having a bit of a kiss and cuddle, but he soon realised the copper didn't believe him so he changed his story to say that he was a minicab driver who'd picked up a fare and had taken a wrong turn.

'Then why,' asked the copper, 'were you sitting in the front of the car with your trousers undone, exposing yourself while this young lady lowered her head towards your groin?' Terry couldn't answer, but he showed the copper his two-way radio to try to add some validity to his story.

The officer laughed. 'The trouble is sir, your 'fiancée' is well known to me and my colleagues down at the nick and she knows more tricks then Harry Houdini.'

He was sent on his way with a warning. After that the only serious relationship he'd had recently was with his right hand.

Today he had marked off a couple of horses that had caught his eye and he carried on studying the form whilst sitting on the toilet for half an hour. The sound of that girl's voice from the advert drifting in from the telly had him pulling his trousers and pants up in a flash as he rushed in from the toilet, 'I'd fuck the arse off that,' he sneered at the screen as he rubbed his crotch, dreaming the girl could see him touching himself. He went back into the toilet to retrieve the newspaper he had dropped in his rush to catch a glimpse of Miss Soap Suds. He laid back into the armchair and flicked through the pages of the paper. He was bored. There was nothing on the telly, the page-three girl's tits weren't big enough to have a wank over, there was no football on last night and so there were no match reports to read about. He folded the paper in half and threw it onto the settee opposite. He counted his books of Green Shield Stamps, but even with the couple of sheets he'd got with yesterday's petrol he still didn't have enough to get anything good from the catalogue. He grabbed his jacket, checked he had some money in his pocket and set off for Mr Singh's shop. As he walked along the balcony he could see an ambulance picking someone up from the playing field.

Alfie, the caretaker, was busy mopping the lift out with a bucket of soapy water.

'Morning Alf.'

'Morning Tel.'

'More trouble Alf?'

'Fucking dirty bastards. I'm sure that the people that piss in these lifts live here in this block, I don't know what's a bleedin' matter with them. Every flat's got its own toilet, so why don't they use it?'

'Animals, Alf, fucking animals. Dirty bastards, that's all they are.'

'After this,' said Alf, 'I've got to go over to the block opposite the pub and scrub some graffiti off of one of the landing walls. The kids have been writing things about that Nigel. You know – the one that lives with his mum.'

'Yeah, I heard about that the other day, ain't he meant to be a bit of a nonce?' Terry replied.

'Anyway, I can't stand around gossiping all day,' Alf said.

'Don't work too hard, Alf.'

'Yeah, see ya Tel.'

Terry decided to give the lifts a miss and walk down the 12 flights of stairs. Struggling down with a pram were Lynn and her three kids.

'Hello sweetheart. Here – let me give you a hand.'

Lynn smiled and thanked him. Terry picked the pram up with her youngest still fast asleep and off he went down the endless damp concrete flights of stairs. He placed the pram down carefully at the bottom, dug his hand into his pocket and fished out a few coins.

'Here you go. Get yourselves some sweets.' He smiled as he handed the money to the children.

'Don't be silly, you don't have to do that.' said Lynn.

Terry smiled and ruffled the kids' hair as they inspected the handful of change he had given them.

'Maybe I'll see you later.'

'Yeah, maybe,' said Lynn as she dashed off, the kids once again late for school.

Terry passed the park where two kids in school uniform, aged about 12 were smoking a fag each whilst swinging backwards and forwards on the swings. Another kid rode round and round on his bike circling them, his arms just long enough to reach the ends of the cow-horn handlebars.

'You'll be late for school,' Terry said, knowing full well they had no intention of going to school. 'You'll have the school inspector after ya.'

'Fuck school,' said the biggest of the two, as he flicked the fag butt he had had in his mouth ten feet into the air with his little finger. Pieces of burning red ash flew in every direction. His mate laughed as the kid on the bike rode over to where it had landed, picked it up and sucked on it to get one last drag out of it before it died.

'You bastard, you promised me the last draw!'

Next stop was Mr Singh's. Despite hostilities by some of the locals, Mr Singh remained, as ever, polite and cheerful and whoever visited the shop got a warm welcome. Mrs Singh sat behind the glass partition of the post office section of the shop. She waved as she served old Mrs Smith her pension. 'Good morning, Terry my good friend, what can I get you?'

Terry walked around the shop consulting the shopping list inside his head. He needed bread, milk, eggs, butter, tea bags, coffee, cornflakes, and a packet of streaky bacon. He loaded up

the wire shopping basket and placed it on the counter in front
of Mr Singh, who rang up the price of each item before putting
them in a plastic carrier bag.

'Twenty Park Drive as well please, Mr Singh.' Mr Singh turned
and took the cigarettes off the shelf. He handed them to Terry.

'Anything else?'

'No, I think that's about everything,' said Terry, unwrapping the
cellophane from the packet of cigarettes, and putting a fag in his
mouth as he handed over a twenty pound note to Mr Singh.

'I notice you've cut yourself shaving. We have some nice-
smelling aftershave on special offer.'

'No thanks,' said Terry, gently dabbing the piece of toilet roll
he'd forgotten he had stuck to his chin.

'How about a gift set I've just got in from the warehouse?
There's aftershave, deodorant, and soap all in a presentation
box, and I'll give it to you at a good price.'

'No thanks,' said Terry, 'I don't need anything like that.'

He picked up the shopping and bid the Singh family farewell.
Next stop was the betting shop, which was a 20-yard stroll
from Mr Singh's shop. The morning sun was out and it was quite
warm. Inside there were already a few familiar faces scanning
the lists of runners and riders pinned to the walls. Terry pulled
a betting slip from the dispenser on the wall, pulled up a stool,
sat down and picked out a couple of dogs he fancied. He
scribbled traps one and six, reverse forecast, and handed the
slip and a five pound note to the woman behind the counter.
He noticed he could see the outline of her bra through her
white cotton blouse. She was 60 if she was a day, with grey
permed hair and a fixed scowl on her face. She was one
miserable bastard. As she lent forward to put Terry's bet
through the machine he could see down her blouse. Blood
rushed from all parts of his body as things stirred in his pants.

He seemed to go into some kind of trance as he took the slip of paper from her. He thanked her and then walked back to his stool in the corner. He seemed to return to the real world when he realised just how desperate he was becoming.

The jockey Lester Piggott rode almost anything in the racing world and Terry would ride anything in the female world. If it had a pair of tits and a fanny, then Terry would be interested. Looks and age didn't come into it. He filled in an each-way Yankee on another slip and took it up to the counter. This time he didn't have a chance to give Miss Happy the once-over.

Gary, a workmate of Terry's from the minicab office came in and they had a chat about work as they both studied the form.

'What's that nurse like you've picked up a couple of times?' he said. Terry smiled.

'She's fucking lovely, and don't get any ideas about asking her out if you get to pick her up, because she's already spoken for.'

'What, you're already in there then?'

'So to speak.' Terry smiled and nodded.

'Shagged it yet?'

'No comment.'

'I suppose you'll be outside the hospital waiting for her when she finishes today, then?' Gary said.

Terry looked up interested. 'Why has she phoned and booked a car?'

'Three o'clock, she wants picking up.'

'Right then, I'm off,' said Terry looking at his watch. The first of his greyhounds had just finished last so he screwed the betting slip up and threw it in the corner. He said goodbye to Gary and waved goodbye to Miss Happy. She stared back with a 'good riddance and get fucked' look.

He made his way home, passing Alf the caretaker carrying a

mop and bucket. 'Fucking dirty fuckers have pissed in another lift over the block opposite the pub, and they've been spitting and pissing down on passers by.'

'I told you Alf, they're worse than dirty animals,' Terry said.

He got home and put his shopping away and made himself a cup of tea. He sat back and watched a bit of telly and it wasn't long before he was sound asleep. He'd only managed to get four hours' kip when he'd got home last night. He lay there for a couple of hours when something in his brain made him stir. He sat bolt upright and looked at his watch. He jumped to his feet, switched the telly off and grabbed his coat along with his money, bag and car keys and was out, slamming the front door behind him. He ran along the walkway. He pressed the button for the lifts, but the light above showed they were both being used on the ground floor.

Fuck it, he thought. I'll have to use the stairs. Off he ran, jumping some of the steps two or three at a time. His heart was pumping and his chest heaving. He checked his watch again, sweat trickling down his brow. He pulled at the door that led from the back entrance of the flats into the rear car park and looked down at the bunch of keys in his hand, picked out the one that would open the car door and was stopped by someone in his way.

'Sorry,' he said and looked up to see Lynn standing there.

'In a hurry are we?' she said.

'Yeah, sorry, can't stop.' As Terry reached the car he fumbled with the key in the lock. He jumped in and started the engine and was off, black smoke trailing behind him. He switched on his two-way radio that linked him to the minicab office. Immediately a voice came over the air.

'Car wanted for a pick up from the hospital, any drivers in the vicinity.' Terry had a good idea who that could be.

'Yeah. Car 22, Terry speaking. I'm less than a minute from the pick up. Over.'

'Job's yours, Tel,' replied the controller. 'You've to pick up one of the nurses and take her home.'

'Yeah, copied that,' said Terry, well pleased he had got the job – even though he had lied and was at least 20 minutes away from the hospital.

When he arrived, his Miss World was waiting for him by the entrance. She looked at the watch on her wrist.

'Sorry I'm late love, but the traffic was horrendous,' said Terry as he lent across and unlocked the front passenger door. She climbed in next to him, conscious of him staring as she got in. Terry pulled out of the hospital and joined the traffic in the nearly empty streets.

'Soon cleared,' Terry smiled. 'Going home?'

'Yes please. I can't wait to get home and a nice shower, something to eat and then bed.' Terry's imagination went into overdrive.

'Let's skip the shower and the food and let's go to bed,' said a voice in his head. If there is such a thing as telepathy, he thought, then let her invite me in. She wound down the window and stuck out her face to let in some fresh air. Being a nurse, she was used to all sorts of human odours, but Terry's lack of personal hygiene was making her feel quite sick. She had spent all night giving bedbaths, clearing up sick, urine and stripping beds covered in blood and shit – but this smell was inches away from her nose and it was turning her stomach.

As Terry drove along and spoke to her he made a point of touching her arm and resting his hand on her leg. Her head was facing into the wind coming through the open window.

'Back to work tonight?' Terry asked, keeping his eyes more on her than the road.

THE ESTATE

'No, I've got the next couple of days off,' she replied, only briefly turning her head to answer him. Terry came straight to the point. In for a penny, in for a pound; shit or bust, he thought – now's my chance, I know she wants it. He pulled the car up outside her house which she shared with some other nurses. He looked at her and she looked at him he composed himself and blurted it straight out.

'Do you fancy coming out for a drink with me one night?' She got out of the car, picked up all her belongings and smiled – not her normal flirty, friendly ear-to-ear smile, more of a smirk.

'You must be fucking joking. I wouldn't be seen dead with a smelly, dirty bastard like you,' she said. Terry's jaw dropped. 'And another thing, keep your sweaty, grubby, filthy, dirty hands to yourself. Touch me one more time and I'll have you done for indecent assault. I'm going straight in to phone your company and tell them never to send you to pick me up again. Have you got the picture?'

Terry slammed the car into gear and roared off. He picked up his radio.

'Car 22 to base.'

'Yes, go ahead, Tel.'

'Yeah, I'm calling it a day. I don't feel well.'

'OK, copied, see ya tomorrow?'

'Yeah, maybe.'

SIX

TAKE ME BACK HOME

'Winston, Winston are you asleep? I need a hand here, there's a customer here that wants served.' Winston stretched his arms above his head, slipped on his flip-flops, let out a loud yawn and stood up from the deck chair where he'd been lying under a palm tree having a snooze. A gentle cooling breeze blew across the sandy bay where Winston and his wife Pam ran their beach bar. 'Sorry darling, I must have dozed off,' he said rubbing his eyes and tucking his short-sleeved shirt back into his shorts. Going behind the bar, he began serving. The place was now heaving with people. When he'd taken a bottle of cold beer and a sandwich outside for a break there had been only one or two regulars in, having a drink and playing a game of dominoes. When he dozed off he had even dreamt that he was back in Britain in the winter, driving a double-decker bus through the cold wind and driving rain. It was more of a nightmare than a dream really, with sleet and snow settling on the slippery roads.

The phone behind the bar rang and he picked it up and

answered. 'Hello, Bayside Diner, how can I help you?' Funny, he had picked the phone up and yet it was still ringing. 'Hello, hello, hello!' he shouted down the line, and yet the ringing tone got even louder. Winston tapped the receiver with the palm of his hand. 'Hello, hello, is someone there?' The tone of the ring changed. It now sounded almost like a bell ringing. Winston's head was now spinning. The sunshine had gone and it seemed he was lying on his back in a dark room. 'Where am I?' he thought as the ringing sound drilled deep inside his brain. He couldn't work out what was going on. Instinctively his arm seemed to be fumbling around in the dark. He felt something made of metal and glass, touched a button and the ringing stopped.

Winston sat up and looked around. He was in bed. The moonlight coming in through the gap in the curtains was the only light in the room. His wife lay fast asleep next to him. He looked at the clock on the bedside cabinet. It was 4.45 a.m. He got up and made his way into the bathroom, where he gently closed the door. He might have to be awake at this unearthly hour, but his wife and son Earl, who was in the next bedroom, didn't. He had a shower and a shave, and as he ran the razor over his face he looked in the mirror and laughed about his Jamaican dream. Before he had gone to bed last night, he and his wife had had another of their many talks about returning to live in the West Indies. Both of them would have good pensions from their jobs when they eventually retired. Pam had worked hard as a midwife and a district nurse for the NHS, and had won many people over with her bubbly personality and enthusiastic attitude to the job. Lots of her patients had become good friends and she still received letters and birthday and Christmas cards from people she had met 20 years ago. For the past ten years she had wanted to give up renting a place from the council and buy a property, nothing too lavish, just somewhere clean and tidy that she would be proud to call home. She wasn't one to be flash; the place she had in mind didn't have to have 20 bedrooms with a tennis court and swimming pool, an end-of-terrace or semi-detached house would do. She would be more than happy as long as she had a nice-sized garden which she could potter about in and grow some flowers.

Winston, on the other hand, believed that any money they managed to save between now and their retirement should be put in a high-interest account and used to buy a house and a bar back in Jamaica. It had always been his dream to return home one day with enough money to run his own beach bar. As a kid, he had dreamt of one day living and working in England. He had seen a book in the school library with pictures of Buckingham Palace and the guards outside in their red tunics and bearskin hats standing to attention as the royal car drove past in it. He read all he could find on British history, and tales of famous battles, castles and kings and queens could engross him for hours. He looked at pictures of Scotland, with men in skirts and mountains covered in snow, something he'd never seen in the West Indies. He had told all of his schoolfriends that one day he would go to England to make his fortune and return home to Jamaica a rich man. Now, 20 years later, he wanted to fulfil his dream and return home. He didn't know about the rich bit, but he had a few bob in his pocket.

He finished in the bathroom, switched off the light and crept downstairs, where he put on his grey suit, white shirt and tie, which were hanging on the back of the kitchen door. He polished his shoes as he waited for the kettle to boil, then slipped them on, drank his tea and picked up his overcoat and inspector's hat from the coatstand in the hallway. He checked he had everything, opened the front door and stepped out on to the landing, closing the door quietly behind him. The leather soles of his shoes tapped on the cold grey concrete flooring. As he walked towards the stairs, he passed the milkman, who mumbled something about delivering to homes in the sky. His dream about sunnier climes came back to him and he laughed, 'beach bar back home to rarse clarte'.

The bus garage Winston worked at was less then a ten-minute drive away, because at this time of the morning the roads were clear. Coming home, the return journey was a different matter and it could take anything up to an hour. Some mornings in the summer when it was light early, he would walk to work. Then his imagination would kick in and he would daydream about walking along a long, golden sandy beach, with palm trees swaying in the breeze, and fishermen unloading their catches as sea gulls hovered overhead for any scraps.

Winston loved to dream about home. He had only been back there once in 20 years, and that was for his gran's funeral. His mum and dad still lived on the island and he hadn't seen them for nearly ten years. His two sons, Earl and Eric, had only seen their grandparents that once, and going to Jamaica had been a real culture shock for the two of them. They were only young at the time and until that trip hadn't realised how well off they were. They saw poverty that they hadn't known existed. Kids played football out in the dusty streets with nothing on their feet and went to school like that as well. Their grandparents lived in what looked like a tin shack, with no electricity or running water and goats and chickens wandering in and out. Most people didn't seem to have proper jobs and what money they did have came from growing a few vegetables, selling eggs or taking one of their animals to market. The two boys couldn't wait to get home. They had missed their friends and playing football and cricket in the park, television and the luxury of hot and cold running water, and going to the shops with their mum and having the choice of hundreds of different kinds of sweets and comics. They couldn't even understand what some of the people they had met there were saying. Were they speaking some kind of strange foreign language? They had sometimes heard their mum and dad speaking the same way, but only if they were angry. No, England was their home and they had no wish to join in their father's dream of returning to live in Jamaica. They were on mum's side on this one – buy a nice house and enjoy retirement in England.

Winston pulled up in the staff car park behind the garage and headed for the manager's office, where Clive, the depot manager, was studying some paperwork. 'Morning Winston,' he said without looking up.

'Morning Clive, how did you know it was me?'

'I've worked here with you for what is it now, ten years, and how many times have you been late? Out of all my senior staff, you're always the first one in on early shift.'

Winston nodded his head in agreement. It was nice to be recognised as a good timekeeper. 'Are you playing cricket on Sunday? It's the big one, our garage against our colleagues from the North London depot.'

'I'll be there,' said Clive, 'and make sure you bring that son of yours along.'

'You mean Earl? I think he's got a football match with the team he plays for on the estate.'

'That boy should be playing cricket, not football. Cricket is in his blood, have you explained that to him?'

'All sports are in his blood. He's like his brother. The only sport he ain't too keen on is swimming, and that's because he's like his old man and has too much rudder.' Winston clutched his crotch and laughed. He grabbed his clipboard and went off into the huge hanger, where all the buses had been parked overnight. Drivers and conductors stood around chatting. Everyone that Winston passed stopped what they were doing and acknowledged him. Known as a fair man who had started at the bottom and worked his way up, he was well liked and respected by everyone. When he had first arrived in this country he had stayed with his mum's brother, who had got him an apprenticeship as a fitter. He had then gone on to get his driving licence and become a bus driver. For the past couple of years he'd been an inspector, and really enjoyed the job.

'Right, come on lads, let's get these buses rolling.'

Within half an hour the garage was almost empty. It was time for some breakfast and so it was off to the staff canteen. He found a table and sat down.

'Usual Winston?' asked Carol, the lady who ran the canteen.

'Yeah, go on then.' He picked up a morning paper somebody had left behind and spread it out across the table. Within minutes, his breakfast of two eggs, bacon, sausage, fresh tomatoes and tea with one sugar and two pieces of toast was laid out in front of him. Carol pulled up a chair and joined him. 'How are you darling?' she asked, looking deep into his eyes. Carol, a divorcee who was game for a laugh, had earned a reputation as a bit of a man-eater; a number of the drivers flirted with her and a few had even asked her out. She often wore low-cut tops that left little to the imagination and short skirts to work and frightened some of the younger members of staff to death. She thought nothing of coming out from behind the counter, delivering someone's breakfast and then hiking her skirt up and sitting on her target's lap. Young boys who took her seriously would go red as a beetroot as she smothered them with kisses while cuddling them and wrapping her arms around their necks. When it was quiet Winston would often flirt with her, and sit and have a chat. They genuinely liked one another.

'Coming to the game on Sunday?' asked Winston.

'Don't know, might do. I don't know what I'm doing yet,' she replied as she picked at her chipped, bright-red nail polish. 'Will your wife be there?' she asked.

Winston chuckled. 'I just asked if you were coming to watch the cricket. I didn't ask if you wanted to sleep with me.'

She stood up and winked. 'The answer is yes to both questions,' she said as she turned and went back to her work.

Winston laughed. If he didn't know her better, he would have sworn she was after him. He rubbed his chin, deep in thought, and folded his newspaper in half. He should know better; she was getting him at it now. He looked across to the counter and she glanced up, smiled and blew him a kiss. 'See you in the showers on Sunday. I'll bring my towel.'

'Rarse clarte,' he said as he buttoned his jacket up. He wiped his mouth with a paper napkin and waved her goodbye.

The shift went fairly smoothly, nothing out of the ordinary. One of the buses wasn't running on time, but with over 50 buses running from the garage on his shift, that wasn't too bad. After work he drove home, peeled some potatoes and put a chicken in the oven, then opened a can of beer and sat in front of the telly to watch the cricket. Earl came in from college and asked who was playing. 'Surrey versus Hampshire,' said his dad as he tapped the space next to him on the sofa. 'Why don't you sit down and watch it with me?'

'No, I've got stacks of homework to do,' replied Earl, studying his new, fashionable Afro hairstyle in the mirror.

'What's with all the big hair?' asked Winston, taking his eyes off the telly for a few seconds. 'Are you trying to look like that family of black kids that were on Top of the Pops the other night? What was their name?' He thought for a while, rubbing his chin. The name came back to him. 'Oh yeah, The Jackson Five, that was them. Rarse clarte, them boys sure had some hair on them. Good singers and dancers though, the little one had a good voice. Still, I bet we'll never hear of them again, just like all those other groups coming over from the States. One-hit wonders, that's what they'll be.'

Earl slammed his bedroom door behind him, mumbling about how embarrassing his dad was, and within seconds music was blaring, drowning out the commentary from the television. Earl flicked through his record collection and wondered what to put on next. Gladys Knight, or Marvin Gaye maybe, Diana Ross or Jimmy Ruffin, the Temptations or Stevie Wonder? No he didn't fancy any of those. He picked up a stack of blue-beat singles, or Ska as the skinheads that had adopted it as their own music were calling it, and placed a Pioneers record, Long Shot Kick the Bucket, on the turntable. He cleaned the needle and lowered the arm onto the spinning disc.

Winston finished his can of Red Stripe and checked how the dinner was doing. The potatoes were done and he turned them off, prepared a salad and put it in the fridge, and turned the chicken over, increasing the temperature of the oven. The front door opened and slammed shut.

'That smells good,' said Pam, taking her coat off and hanging it in the hallway.

Winston gave his wife a welcoming kiss. 'How was work?'

'Fine.'

'Dinner will be ready in fifteen minutes.'

'Fine, let me get out of this uniform. Winston, tell Earl to turn that music down will you please? I could hear it as I got out of the lift.'

'I've tried telling him, but he can't hear me.' Winston made his wife a cup of tea and put it on the coffee table. Earl appeared from his room and made himself a drink of squash. 'Dinner is nearly ready son, and Mum said can you turn that music down. How on earth can you study with all that noise?'

Earl looked at him and shook his head. 'Dad, you're showing your age.' The two of them laughed.

'How was that?' asked Winston after dinner, looking at his wife as he pushed his plate into the middle of the table. Pam stacked the three empty plates on top of one another.

'What's for pudding Mum?' Earl asked.

'Your favourite, apple pie and fresh cream.'

Winston leant forward and took a toothpick from the glass pot in the middle of the table. He sucked his teeth, making a sound like a budgie calling for his mate as he cleaned the inside of his mouth with his tongue, trying to remove bits of chicken from the gaps in his teeth. 'There's a cricket match this Sunday, Earl. I wondered if you fancied playing,' he said hopefully.

'I can't, Dad. I'm playing for the Tavern, we've got a big cup game and we're just one game away from the final, so I don't want to miss it. Otherwise I would.'

Pam placed the dessert on the table, but before she could sit down to enjoy it the phone rang. 'Hello, darling. How are you, long time no hear, how are the children, give them a kiss from me, and say hello to Jane.'

'Must be your brother, because he can't get a word in,' said Winston, tucking into his apple pie. The family hadn't seen Eric for a couple of months. He was married with a couple of children, and was serving in the British Army as a physical training instructor. He loved his job and was stationed up in Yorkshire, where his wife came from. Like his dad and younger brother, he was sports mad. When he was younger he had been a good boxer, footballer and cricket player and his careers master at school had suggested that he joined the army and see the world. The idea had stuck, and the rest was history.

'Yes, yes, I'll tell your dad. We'll all be pleased to see you. Yeah, take care darling, I'll see you on Friday night.'

'Winston, that was Eric. He's coming to stay this weekend. Isn't that good news?'

A grin spread across Winston's face. If Earl couldn't make the cricket match, then he was sure Eric would turn out for the garage. Pam saw him smiling. 'If you're thinking what I think you're thinking, then you can get the idea out of your head straight away. He's coming to visit his family, not run round some cricket pitch.'

'Yes dear,' said Winston, knowing full well that Eric would like nothing more than to play alongside his dad. The last time the pair had played together Eric had been 160 not out, while his dad got a half-century. Most county cricket clubs would willingly sign Eric up as a full-time player.

On the day of the match the sun was shining and a good crowd had gathered. A few people were stretched out on the grass drinking wine, one or two of them sprawled out on checked picnic blankets. The pitch was in excellent condition, dry and firm. Winston and Eric were to be the opening bats. The opposition's fielders took up their positions. As the pair strode onto the field, their bats under their arms, a round of applause came from the pavilion.

They wished each other luck as they parted. Winston looked around to see where the fielders had positioned themselves. He was to receive the first ball and was feeling nervous – he just wanted to get the first ball out of the way. He checked his gloves and pads and adjusted his grip slightly. He stood at his crease and tapped the bat on the grass to flatten any divots, then watched as the bowler turned and walked away to the far end. He was taking a fair old run-up.

The umpire held his arm out to his side to tell the bowler he was not ready yet. He checked that the scorekeepers were ready, checked that Winston was ready and then dropped his arm to signal that play could start. The bowler rubbed the red ball on his white flannels, leaving a mark just below his groin, then came running towards Winston, hop, skip and jumping as he released it. The ball flew towards Winston's crease. It was a spinning bouncer. Winston watched the ball all the way and could picture himself hitting it for a four or even a six. It bounced and spun. Winston adjusted his back foot, moved one step forward and adjusted the line of his bat slightly so that he caught the ball just right.

'WINSTON!' someone in the crowd shouted and he took his eye off the flight of the ball and turned to see Carol calling out and waving to him. As he looked behind, he could see the stumps flying into the air. 'YES!' the opposition shouted as the wicket-keeper threw the ball into the air. The umpire smiled, nodded and pointed towards the pavilion as Winston, head bowed, walked off.

SEVEN

TINKERS AND TRAVELLERS AND TROUBLEMAKERS

'Did you hear that Boxer John is going to fight Johnny Cream this Sunday over on the site?'

'John will fucking kill him.'

'Bollocks, you're talking out of your arse, there's not been a man born from his mother that could beat that man. He's the finest bare-knuckle fighter you're ever likely to see.'

'I'll have a bet widge yas.'

'You're on, and you and 400 other travelling folk will all be proved wrong.'

'Billy Boy, do us a favour and run over to the Paki shop and get some milk, your father wants a cup of tea.'

'I can't,' said Billy Boy, his hands down his pants playing with his todger as he sat glued to the television. 'That Paki man has barred me, Sean and Jimmy boy for choring.'

'Right Johnny Boy, you'll have to take me to the supermarket in town.'

'But Mum, I'm watching telly.'

'No buts, I'm fucking fed up with buts, every time I ask you two to do anything it's "but this" and "but that". I asked you to feed the two Shetlands in the back garden this morning and you went off without doing it. Come on you pair of lazy bastards, you can both come with me. Jim, give us some money.'

Jim pulled a crumpled wad of notes from his back pocket and peeled off a couple from the large, tightly wrapped bundle in his hand. 'Get me some fags and a couple of bottles of brown ale, will ya please, luv.'

Mrs O'Hara pulled on her coat and shouted at her two boys to get their fucking arses into gear. Both boys quickly slipped their shoes on and Billy tucked his shirt into his opened trousers and zipped them up. 'You'll pull your fucking dick off boy, all you fucking do is play with it while you're watching that poxy telly.' Billy smiled as his mother hollered at them again to hurry up.

Johnny and his mother and brother all squeezed into the front of the open-backed truck, which was loaded up with scrap metal of all descriptions. There were gas cookers, fridges, washing machines, lead pipes, copper tubing, car batteries, cast iron guttering and bags of rags and old clothes. The boys had had a good day out on their rounds, calling around the streets ringing their bell, and searching through rubbish skips. They had scoured disused factories and building sites for old iron and other metal, in fact anything worth salvaging which could be sold on for a few quid.

The O'Haras were what most people would call rag-and-bone men or 'totters'. They'd moved onto the estate after travelling around the country from site to site in their caravan. Mum Katie and Dad Jim, along with their five boys, Johnny, Billy, Jimmy, Sean and Joe and their daughter Kayleigh-Louise had originally come to settle in England from their native Ireland where, because they were gypsies, they felt they were being persecuted by the garda and local government officials. Since their arrival in England they'd made a living from scrap metal, roofing and tarmacing drives. Their daughter had got married last year and they hadn't seen her since her wedding day. Family and friends had travelled from all parts of the country to be there. They had a big white wedding with a reception at a pub afterwards for 300 guests. The beer flowed and the music played, or at least until a punch-up started between the guests. Glasses and bottles, and tables and chairs were smashed and broken, many of them over people's heads. The police were called to restore order and a few of the guests were arrested for being drunk and disorderly. The landlord of the pub was left with a huge clearing-up bill and an unpaid bar tab of nearly two thousand pounds. It took the council another six weeks to get the 50 families and their caravans moved off the field they were living on. Since that day Kayleigh had refused to have anything to do with her family, because she blamed them for ruining her big day. It turned out that her father had started an argument with the groom about looking after his daughter. The man had taken exception to how he was being spoken to and told his father-in-law in no uncertain terms to mind his own fucking business. Kayleigh's dad had laid the man out with one punch, then blacked the boy's father's eye, before all hell broke loose.

The eldest boy, Joe, was presently serving a five-year sentence in one of Her Majesty's prisons on the Isle of Wight. He had been found guilty of overcharging an old lady for work he had carried out on her roof. He had originally quoted her two hundred pounds to replace some tiles and to cement some ridge tiles back into place, but by the time he and his mate had finished the work, the cost had risen dramatically and they'd presented the old girl with a bill for two thousand, five hundred pounds. To justify this they said they'd had to replace the back gutters and down pipes and had repointed her storm-damaged chimney stack, which they told her was ready to come crashing in around her head. The old lady told them she didn't keep that sort of money in the house, and that she wanted her son to inspect any work carried out before she parted with the money. The boys' reply to that was if she didn't pay that day, then they were quite within their rights to remove any work they had carried out, or to charge double for every day that full payment was not received. The old dolly was scared shitless. 'What happens if you remove the tiles you've put in and it rains tonight?' she had asked, worried that she might not have a house standing the next morning.

'Then you get wet, your ceilings will get soaked and collapse, and besides the mess and the cost of having a plasterer in, your bill would have doubled,' said Joe, turning his face away so that she couldn't see him trying to stop himself from bursting out laughing.

'Have you a bank account?' asked his mate, acting as if he cared about the old girl's welfare.

'Yes,' she replied.

'Well, I'll tell you what we can do. We'll run you down to the bank and you can withdraw the money. We won't even charge you any extra, that's just part of our service. You see, we like to make sure our customers are happy and satisfied.'

Joe had then run the old lady down to the bank to make her withdrawal while his mate stayed behind and ransacked her house. He found her jewellery box in the bedroom and emptied it, and took what little cash she had from an old teapot she kept in one of her kitchen cupboards. Joe told her that if anyone at the bank questioned what she was doing, she should tell them that Joe was her nephew and that she was going to buy him a car, hence the large withdrawal. The girl behind the counter knew the old lady. She was a bit suspicious and said she would have to speak to the manager first before she could release such a large sum of money without prior notice. Joe pointed out that it was his auntie's savings and it was up to her what she spent her money on, and told the girl she should mind her own business. After all, she was only a bank clerk. If his auntie wanted to withdraw her savings to buy her favourite nephew a car, it had nothing to do with anyone else. Nevertheless the girl went off to see the manager. But she was back within seconds. 'The manager has someone with him at the moment, so you will either have to wait or come back some other time.'

The old girl, who had hardly said a word, suddenly piped up in Joe's defence. He couldn't believe it. 'I've been banking here for over 40 years. I've never been overdrawn and I am on first name terms with the manager and most of the staff. Now if you would be so kind, I would like to withdraw two thousand, five hundred pounds.'

'But Mrs Brunswick, I'm only . . .'

'Now, if you would be so kind,' the old lady repeated and handed over her bank book. The girl slipped open the drawer behind the counter and counted out the money. Mrs Brunswick signed the slip of paper while the clerk handed over the money and returned her bank book with the money neatly counted and folded inside. 'Good day to you,' said the old girl as she handed the money over to her jubilant new family member. Back at the house, Joe and his mate quickly loaded up the van and had it away a bit lively. Unbeknown to them, a neighbour across the road from the old lady had not only taken the registration number of the van, but had also taken photos of Joe and his mate from his bedroom window. Within days, the old bill knew exactly who they were looking for. They had the van registration, a security video from the bank, fingerprints from the teapot and the neighbour's photos. On the very day the family stopped travelling and moved into their house on the estate they were down one family member; Joe was arrested and charged with deception and his mate with burglary. His dad Jim blamed himself. It was his idea initially to stop travelling and to apply for a council place. 'If we weren't stuck in this house, our Joe wouldn't be banged up, doing a bit of bird.' The rest of the family had tried to convince their dad that it wasn't his fault.

Jim's parents had also stopped travelling and had moved in right next door to them, in one of the purpose-built homes set aside for elderly or disabled people. They'd been given the house by mistake, due to a mix-up at the council. They should have had a one-bedroom flat in one of the tower blocks, but because someone had not done their job properly they now had a two-bedroom bungalow.

The battered truck pulled into the supermarket car park and the O'Haras got out. Not one of them bothered to wind the windows up, or even lock the doors. Billy even left the cassette playing, with the sound of Johnnie Cash singing about a gal from Texas echoing around the car park.

'Bill, get one of them barrows.'

'Bollocks, I ain't going to make myself look stupid,' he said, studying his Elvis hairstyle in the cracked wing mirror of the truck while standing well back from the shopping trolley, as if it might give him an electric shock if he touched it.

'Just get one will ya for fuck's sake,' said Mum angrily. Bill grabbed one and looked around to see if anyone in the crowds of shoppers were laughing or sniggering at him. He stared at people, paranoid, almost daring them to catch his eye and laugh at him to his face.

They passed a security guard at the front door who gave them the once-over before turning his head to the side and speaking into his radio, which was on the lapel of his dark-blue jacket. His eyes followed them into the store. They were well known to him and he knew they were trouble.

As they passed the fruit, Billy picked up a shiny red apple and bit into it, pieces of it flying from his mouth as he spoke. 'Fucking handsome.' Johnny helped himself to a handful of black cherries while Mum sorted herself out with a nice juicy pear. Gypsy folk call this grazing. They loaded various items into the trolley, but some things, like a large joint of beef, went into Mum's shopping bag. Bill picked up a bar of chocolate, snapped it in half and put one piece into his mouth and the other into his pocket. Meanwhile his brother was tucking into some chocolate Brazil nuts.

The security man appeared and followed them at a distance down each aisle. They began to have a bit of a game with him; Mum would pick up a bottle of spirits from the drinks section and pretend to be looking around to see if anyone was watching. With the guard's attention hooked, she'd then walk away with it still in her hands. The security man, thinking she was thieving, would follow her all the way to the exit, where at the last moment she would turn round, retrace her steps and put the bottle back on the shelf. As she turned from the door the security guard, only feet behind her, nearly tripped over as he bumped straight into her. 'Sorry my love,' she said as the red-faced man stepped out of the way.

Billy and Johnny were meanwhile pushing the loaded shopping trolley out through the main doors, bypassing the checkouts. No one gave them a second look. They lifted the shopping trolley with all their groceries inside straight onto the back of the truck. With Mum safely beside them they roared out of the car park, their weekly shopping done.

'Mum, the minicab is here,' Billy shouted up the stairs to his mum, who was putting the finishing touches to her hair in the bathroom mirror. Mum and Gran were off to the Isle of Wight to visit Joe in prison. Mrs O'Hara had chatted up Terry the cab driver and persuaded him to do the journey for a fixed price. Dad, Jim and the boys, along with their granddad, Jim senior, were doing a clearance job for a local builder. If all went well they could come out with five hundred pounds each today. The plan was that they'd fill Dad's and Johnny's trucks up with rubbish from a building site, but instead of taking it to the council dump, where they'd have to pay, they'd sneakily tip it down a quiet lane on the other side of town and it would cost nothing, so their scam would be all profit.

Mum and Gran came out of the house and climbed into the back of Terry's car. The boys and their father stopped loading shovels and wheelbarrows onto their trucks and leant in through the back window of the car to give Mum and Gran a kiss goodbye in turn. 'Give my love to Joe Boy,' they all shouted as the car pulled away and turned out of the quiet close and into the distance.

There was an awful smell in the cab. Mum wound down the window and asked Terry what it was. He went bright red and made up a story about a man he'd picked up on his last job, who had been taking a greyhound dog to the vets. He embellished the story further by saying that the dog's mother had once won the Greyhound Derby. One thing gypsies didn't like was sharing their space with dogs, even if they were champions. Unlike gorgers (the name given to non-gypsies), travellers will not have any animals inside their homes.

Within half an hour Gran was fast asleep and only woke up when they reached the ferry terminal at Portsmouth harbour. 'Oh, I must have dozed off,' she yawned. Mrs O'Hara looked at Terry and they both laughed. 'Must be the age,' she said.

On board the boat the women stretched their legs, then sat in the restaurant and had a pot of tea and a sandwich. Terry said he didn't travel too well on boats and claimed to feel a bit seasick, even though the ferry hadn't left the port yet. He decided to stay in the car on the journey across and read his paper and study the horses. On the other side it was only a fifteen-minute journey to the prison, and once there, Terry parked up and waited in the car while they walked across to the main gates.

The last time they had made the trip they had gone by train and had had a nightmare journey. The train had taken forever to get to Portsmouth, something to do with signal failure and track repairs, and then the ferry couldn't leave the harbour due to bad weather. When they did get across, they had waited an hour for a cab to pick them up. They had arrived at the prison late and what should have been an hour's visit only lasted ten minutes. They explained what had happened to the warders, but their requests to stay longer were met with 'you know the rules'.There was just enough time to quickly kiss and cuddle Joe, buy him a cup of tea and ask him if all was well before a screw strolled over and told them to finish up because it was time to go. They asked if they could see the governor to explain about their horrendous journey, but a screw with his peaked cap pulled nearly to the bridge of his pointed nose told them the governor did not meet visitors personally, and if they had any queries or complaints they should put them in writing, either to the governor himself or, if they needed to go higher, to the Home Secretary. Mrs O'Hara stared deep into his eyes. She felt like punching him. He stood with his arms behind his back, chest puffed out. 'You fucking bigheaded awkward cunt, we're gypsies and we can't read or write, so how the fuck are we going to take it up with the Home fucking Secretary?' The screw looked back at Mrs O'Hara and smirked.

THE ESTATE

Today they were at the front of the queue outside the main gates of the prison with plenty of time to spare. After a few minutes they could hear activity on the other side of the wall, keys jangling and doors unlocking as a prison officer appeared and led everyone through into a waiting room, where they handed over their visiting orders and sat down to wait.

Mrs O'Hara and Gran were then asked by an officer to wait behind while everyone else was led away to be searched. 'What's going on?' asked a concerned Mrs O'Hara. 'Has something happened to my son?' A high-ranking prison officer appeared from a side office, backed by a dozen other screws. He stepped forward and spoke. 'Mrs O'Hara, you cannot visit your son here today as he was moved first thing this morning to a prison over on the mainland. He is now residing at Her Majesty's Prison Wandsworth.'

'You fucking wankers, you knew we would be coming all this way to visit him, yet no one had the decency to let us know.'

'These things do happen,' smiled the screw, pleasure evident in his sarcastic tones.

'This is all to do with the last time we were here.' Gran burst into tears.

'Don't let these tossers see you cry Mum, they ain't worth it,' said Mrs O'Hara as she helped her mum back to her feet, out of the prison and back across the road to where Terry's car was parked.

'You're back quick,' said Terry. 'Is Joe all right?'

Mrs O'Hara looked at him, tears welling up in her eyes. 'He ain't there, they've moved him.'

Terry started the car and pulled out of the car park, not knowing what to say. The journey back to the ferry was completely silent. Terry tried to break the ice. 'While I was waiting for you outside the prison a warder with an Alsatian dog came up to me and asked me what I was doing. I think he thought I was in on an escape attempt.' He laughed nervously as there was no response from the two women in the back. The journey back from Portsmouth was like returning from a funeral. Not a word was said. Mrs O'Hara cried buckets of tears, while old Gran looked straight ahead, seeming to be almost in a trance.

'Here we go,' Terry said, 'home at last,' as he pulled up outside the O'Hara's house. They had left that morning at 8 a.m. and it was now 5 p.m. Jim's and the boy's trucks were parked up outside, along with a caravan with a petrol generator chugging away. 'Who parked that trailer there?' asked Mrs O'Hara. As she spoke a head looked round the door. 'I thought I could hear your voice,' said Katie's younger sister Molly cuddling them both. 'Have you two been crying?'

'Looks like the men are back,' said Gran, coming back to life and pointing at the truck.

This prompted more tears from Mrs O'Hara, who was now worried about what the rest of the family would say. 'Wait till they find out what's happened.'

Terry helped them to the door, carrying their bags and placing them on the doorstep. Mrs O'Hara put the key in the lock and stepped inside. She could see down the hallway her son Billy lying on the sofa fast asleep, the telly blaring and flickering away in the corner, and a bottle of empty champagne lying on its side on the floor next to him. She shook him and he stirred and looked up at her.

'Have you been drinking?'

'Yes, Ma.'

'Where did you get the champagne?'

'I found it.'

'Found it my arse, where's your father?' she asked, as Billy sat up rubbing his sore head, his brain only now registering that he had a hangover.

'He's gone to the pub in town with Uncle Henry and a few of the lads.'

'I'll fucking kill him,' she said.

Terry, still waiting outside, called from the front door, 'I'll be off then Mrs O'Hara.'

'Yes, thank you Terry,' she said. 'I'll come and see you in a couple of days and sort your money out.' Gran walked along the passageway. 'Thanks love,' she said, shutting the door in his face. He stood there lost for words, staring at the glass in the front door.

'A couple of days,' he said as he turned and walked away. 'I think I've been well and truly turned over.'

EIGHT

NIGEL'S NIGHTMARE

'Nigel, come away from that window – I know you're watching those kids down there on those swings.' Nigel picked up his coat from where it was hanging in the hallway, slowly opened the front door, stuck his head out and looked both ways to see if the coast was clear.

'Right Mum,' he said. 'I'll see you later.' He closed the door behind him and he made his way quickly along the balcony to the lobby where the lifts were. Someone had sprayed on the wall in red paint, KILL THE NONCE in three-foot-high letters. He decided it would be wise not to wait for one of the lifts and instead opted to take the stairs. It was 9.30 a.m. and most of the kids that made Nigel's life hell would be at school. Recently he had been ambushed in one of the lifts by four men and was beaten so badly that he ended up in hospital for nearly a month. In the attack he had suffered a broken arm, collar bone and nose, and he had been treated for cuts and bruises. He had also been doused in petrol and told that if he didn't get off the estate, then they would come back with a box of matches and finish the job. Despite police enquiries, no witnesses could be found and no one was ever arrested for the attack.

Nigel had a 10 a.m. appointment with the housing officer at the council this morning and instead of waiting for the bus outside the block where he lived, he decided to walk. He couldn't take the chance of waiting in the street in broad daylight – God knows what could happen. It was possible a car could pull up and he would be dragged off and attacked or killed, or some out-of-work teenagers would see him and give him a good kicking. Since the last attack he was a bundle of nerves. Nigel had moved onto the estate with his disabled mother and they should have moved straight into a two-bedroomed bungalow with wheelchair access via ramps to the front and back of the property. Its kitchen had been converted with low-level cupboards and work surfaces and a special bath and shower. But due to an administration error at the council, this bungalow was given over to Mr and Mrs O'Hara senior, and the flat they were supposed to have had was given to Nigel and his mum. When Nigel turned up at the bungalow with the removal men and all their possessions the O'Hara clan had already moved in, and since that day they had refused to budge. A red-faced council officer had been summoned to sort the problem out, but they had refused to move. The council had even issued a court order for their eviction, but the O'Haras said they had done nothing wrong and were still in the process of contesting it. All they had done was to move into the property they had been allocated, and were quite happy where they were, thank you. In other words the council could go and get fucked. The only accommodation available on the estate was the flat meant for the O'Haras, so Nigel and his mum had no option but to move in there and wait for their bungalow to become empty or better still for something else to come along.

Since his assault, Nigel had wanted to move out – anywhere,

so long as it was away from the estate. Today he was hoping that Mrs Willis, the housing officer dealing with his case, would have some news about a move. He and his mum had put their names down for an exchange with someone else, and the way things were, any part of the country would do. They had no other family besides one nephew and his family who they very rarely saw, so they had no ties to anywhere in particular. A place on the coast would be nice, so maybe today he may have some good news for a change. Nigel's life had been turned upside down after just a few months of living on the estate. He didn't work and was paid by the state to be his mum's full-time carer.

Apart from the mix-up with the bungalow everything else had been fairly rosy – that was until a mate from the past, Sid, had unexpectedly turned up.

A few years ago Nigel had got into a bit of bother with the police and had subsequently served a two-year jail sentence. A bloke he had befriended while he was inside suddenly turned up out of the blue. He had gone to Nigel's old address not knowing that he had moved. The young girl and her boyfriend who now lived there didn't have a forwarding address for Nigel but they seemed to have a good idea that he and his mum had moved onto the new estate on the other side of town. Well, Sid wouldn't give up and after a bit of detective work, he found out where Nigel was living. At first no one he asked could help him or point him in the right direction so he decided to have a pint in the local pub. He asked Dave who was working this particular day behind the bar if he'd ever come across Nigel. Dave shook his head and told him that the name don't ring any bells, but the description Sid had given him fitted a bloke that was living with his mother in one of the tower blocks. Dave then phoned Mr Singh and asked him if he could help. When he came back off the phone he said, 'I think you may be in luck. If it is your mate, then he lives on the third floor at number 22 Guildford Court.'

'Right I'll have another pint and a double whisky chaser, and have one for yourself,' said Sid, well pleased that his search may well be coming to an end. Six rounds of drinks later and this 'friend' was still in the pub. Since it was a quiet night, and he didn't have a lot to do, Dave was matching him round for round. After a while Dave began to get inquisitive as to why this man was so keen to meet up with Nigel again. He could sense there was more to this than the man was letting on. Dave asked Sid outright about the search for his mate. With his speech slurring Sid looks around the near empty pub and checks that no one is within earshot. He lifts up his glass and downs the whisky in one, takes another quick look around the pub, then coughs and stares at Dave, his voice just above a whisper, and his lips dead still like a ventriloquist's. He mumbles one word: 'porn.'

'What about it?' asks Dave as he pushes Sid's glass under the whisky optic and hands him a refill.

'My mate Nigel's into porn.'

'Aren't we all?' said Dave, as a man walks past them on his way to use the gents toilet. The conversation stops for a few seconds before Sid looks around to check there is nobody else about.

'Nigel specialises in a certain kind of porn,' Dave smiles and nods at him as if he knows where the man is coming from. The conversation again stops but another large whisky gets his tongue moving again.

'What sort of porn are we talking about here?' asks Dave talking out of the side of his mouth. 'Hardcore, orgies, couples, lesbians, animals, snuff?'

'He did have some good contacts in Holland.'

'What do you mean he did have?' asked Dave, interested.

'Well, when he got put away for indecently assaulting them children.'

'What, you mean he's a child molester?' asked Dave, stepping back away from the bar as if Sid was going to infect him with some deadly disease.

'Well, yeah,' said Sid, sensing he may have said too much.

'Right drink up and fuck off,' said Dave.

'Why what have I done? I thought we were having a nice sensible drink together.'

'We were until you told me that you and your mate were a couple of perverts.' Dave snatched the glass from Sid's hand and told him to get out.

Within hours the news that a child molester was living on the estate had spread, and by the next morning the first piece of graffiti had been sprayed on the wall where Nigel lived. That evening Nigel had dog shit posted through his letter box. After that if he was seen out by mothers with their children they would cross over the road. People of all ages would shout abuse at him, he was a marked man. On the night when he was assaulted he had been across to the fish and chip shop to get his mum and himself some supper. A boy of about fifteen, stood behind him in the queue in a black leather biker's jacket with TRIUMPH spelt out on the back with silver metal studs, made a comment about him. All Nigel had done was to completely ignore him; the next thing he knew he was being confronted by the boy's father outside the shop. The man accused Nigel of making lurid and suggestive remarks towards his boy. Nigel shook his head and walked away. The crowd which had gathered followed him across the road and pushed him up against the wall outside the lifts, 'Kill him!' shouted one of the adults. The next thing he knew, he had been punched to the ground and was being viciously beaten and kicked, he even remembered a woman standing over him and sticking the boot in. He came round in hospital the following morning. The doctor told him he was lucky to be alive. He was only saved by a passer-by who phoned for an ambulance. He was told he could have bled to death. His mum had been frantic with worry and had no idea what had happened to him. A policeman had called around to the flat just after midnight, but she was frightened to open the front door. He had returned around eight the following morning and told her of her son's ordeal.

On his walk to the council office Nigel took a short cut through a nearby park. A river flowed through the park and he stopped by it for a few minutes to listen to the birds singing. The branches of the tree swayed and the sun shone high in the sky. Nigel felt relaxed and unzipped his jacket and stood on the riverbank. Swans and ducks swam past, it was an idyllic scene. For a few moments he had forgotten his troubles. If only life could be this peaceful all the time, he thought to himself. He sat down on the grass and memories of yesteryear began to flood back. His childhood; his strict father; how at 16 he had joined the Royal Air Force, along with his older brother Charles – who had sadly died along with his wife in a tragic car accident only last year. Nigel served 20 years, and his brother 21 years, in the RAF, and thinking back, they were the best years of his life. He had originally joined up to get away from his father. His brother was already serving and told him of the lifestyle he was enjoying. After he had left the services, he found it hard to adjust to civvy street. It was a few years after leaving that he got into trouble with the police. A group of kids that lived near his flat would hang around the front door. Nigel foolishly started to invite some of them in and what began as just a bit of company for him, turned more sinister when he exposed himself to one of the kids and took photos of one of them in the nude. He was arrested, taken to court and found guilty and served 18 months of a two-year sentence. During his time inside he was segregated from the rest of the prison population and spent most of his sentence in a wing that housed rapists, child molesters and police informers. He had shared his cell with a bloke from up north who had got a ten-year sentence for the buggery of a ten-year-old boy. He seemed to get excited and would get off on telling Nigel all the gory details of the case. Compared to the beating Nigel had recently received, he had got off lightly compared to his cellmate. Like Nigel his cellmate had also been cornered and viciously attacked by a gang of vigilantes. They had beaten him to a pulp and when he was knocked unconscious they ripped his trousers and pants off of him and one of the gang then smashed a milk bottle over his head and proceeded to ram it up his arse. He was repeatedly kicked and punched and left for dead. The three men were all charged with attempted murder, but all walked free after a lengthy court case.

Nigel lay back on the grass with his eyes closed. In the distance he could hear voices. They got closer. He first sat up and then quickly stood up when he saw a group of youths, some of whom he recognised from the estate, coming towards him. For a few seconds he was frozen to the spot – he had felt this kind of fear on more than one occasion, panic spread all over his body.

'Look, there's the nonce!' shouted one of the youths waving a stick in the air. 'Get him – yeeehah!'

Nigel was off and running full-pelt for his life.

He followed the path along the riverbank, he didn't look around but he could hear the sound of running feet not that far behind him and they were getting nearer. The park gate and safety was at least half a mile away and there was no way he was going to make it as far as there. His heart was pumping and his chest was tight, as his lungs struggled to take in air. He was slowing down and his legs were getting heavy as sweat poured down his brow. A hand grabbed his shoulder and he could feel someone's breath on his neck.

'I've got you, you fucking nonce.'

Nigel struggled free and without looking, jumped feet-first into the dark brown fast-flowing river. The water came up to his waistline as he waded across to the other side. He clambered up the muddy bank there and stared back over at his pursuers who were standing there laughing and shouting and throwing stones and sticks. He recognised all of them. One of them had a black leather jacket on and he was the boy who had gone and got his dad to beat him up for no reason. Nigel knew it would make matters worse if he said anything and so he turned and walked away. As he left the park and trudged through town people looked at him rather strangely.

The electric doors opened and Nigel trooped in leaving a trail of water that had dripped from his trousers. His shoes squeaked and squelched as he approached the enquiry desk.

'How can I help you?' asked the lady as she looked down her glasses at him.

'I've an appointment with Mrs Willis.'

'I'll let her know you're here, please take a seat.'

'I'd better not, I'm a bit wet.'

The receptionist looked at Nigel and at the trail of water leading from the front entrance. Mrs Willis appeared, shook Nigel's hand and asked him to follow her into the office. Nigel explained what had just happened and said he'd rather stand up than get the chair wet. Standing with water dripping onto the royal-blue carpet he went on to explain what he and his mother had been through since it had been discovered that he was a paedophile. Nigel gave her dates and times of various incidents that had happened to him and his flat. He pulled a damp, crumpled piece of paper from his jacket pocket. He cleared his throat and read out what he had written down.

'Monday: dead rat tied to our letterbox by its tail. Tuesday: lighted newspaper pushed through the letterbox. Wednesday: used condom pushed through the letterbox. Thursday: dog mess pushed through the letterbox and human excrement smeared over our kitchen window.' Mrs Willis couldn't help herself from smiling.

'Friday: a piss-stained mattress dumped on the balcony right outside my front door, and white spirit thrown up the front door and a lighted match put to it.'

'I think I've heard enough,' said Mrs Willis as she held her hand up for Nigel to stop. She thanked him for keeping a diary of sorts, and she scribbled something on a piece of headed notepaper she had in front of her and looked up. 'You have my deepest sympathy for how you and your mother are being treated by certain people and we will be doing our utmost to quickly push through a move to the bungalow which was originally allocated to you. As you well know there is a case being heard in the local courts this week to gain the eviction of a certain family who are illegally squatting in one of our properties, so until such time as that property becomes free, then I'm afraid there is nothing we can do to help you.'

Nigel shook his head in disbelief. 'I can't believe what I'm hearing,' he said. 'I don't think you realise just what me and my mother are going through. My mother is in a wheelchair and these scumbags who keep horses in their back garden and allow their dogs to roam the estate, scavenging in people's dustbins for scraps of food, are allowed to stay in what is mine and my mother's rightful home.'

THE ESTATE

'Well,' she said, 'the only alternative is for you and your mother to maybe look to rent a property privately or maybe even consider buying something.'

In anger Nigel tore up his piece of paper and placed it on the desk in front of Mrs Willis. 'Thanks a lot,' he said as he stormed out.

The next morning Nigel received a letter. He knew it wasn't from the council because the postmark read 'Hemel Hempstead'. He opened it and to his surprise it was from his nephew, Douglas. He hadn't seen or heard from him since his brother Charles and his wife's (Douglas's mum and dad) funeral. The one thing both men had in common was that they liked looking at child porn – and although Douglas was now married, when they did meet up they'd still swap magazines and pictures of kids.

'Give my love to Gran,' he wrote in the letter. Nigel showed it to his mum and also a photograph of Douglas with his wife and their three children.

'He still looks a creep – look at him with that shaven head and those bulging cod-like eyes. He's one shifty-looking git.'

'But he's married now mum,' said Nigel.

'That don't mean nothing – and she's just as bad, the fat bastard, them dresses she squeezes into, two sizes too small, she thinks she's thinner then she is, and them kids they've permanently got colds, with snails' trails leading down from their noses, and when you tell them they cuff it on the back of their sleeves, and when was the last time they bathed, they stink like stale biscuits.'

'Stale biscuits?' laughed Nigel unsure of what his mother meant.

' BO, that's what I mean, they're unwashed,' she said.

'Anyway what's he want? He only comes to see us when he's after something.'

96

Nigel excitedly counted the days down to the weekend of Dougie's visit. He knew why he was coming, and that was to talk about their Dutch venture again. Douglas had been in on Nigel's regular excursions to Amsterdam where they had both made a bob or two from their little scam. They'd go off together for the weekend, buy up cine-films, books, photos and magazines, then come back and sell them to various friends who were interested in child porn. They had many professional people on their books including doctors, dentists, pilots, policemen, judges, barristers and solicitors, right through to dustmen and traffic wardens. Business had been booming until Nigel's arrest. Douglas didn't have the bottle to carry on alone. Nigel knew there was more to this 'social' visit.

Sunday morning came and Nigel had been up early dusting, hoovering and generally tidying up. The doorbell rang and he could see the shapes of people through the frosted glass of the front door.

'Dougie!' he said as his nephew stepped inside the flat and onto the mat with WELCOME on it. Nigel threw his arms around him and hugged and kissed his wife. Dougie introduced the three children who weren't exactly sure who Uncle Nigel was. They had puzzled looks on their faces. They had all been so small when Nigel had seen them last.

'And this is your Great-Gran,' said Dougie as Nigel's mum wheeled herself down the hallway towards them. The children stood and looked.

'Say hello,' said their father.

'Hello,' they all said together, somewhat embarrassed.

Everyone crowded into the tiny lounge and Nigel made tea for them all. Mum chatted to Dougie's wife and filled her in on the mix-up with the flat.

The kids sat on the sofa not moving or saying a word. 'Can we go downstairs and play on the swings?' piped up the eldest one.

'No you can't,' said their mother. 'There are some strange men around and they might take you away.' As soon as she'd come out with it she realised what she had said. 'I'm sorry,' she said, 'I didn't think.'

Nigel's face turned red and Mum smiled. 'That's all right love.'

'I'm just going upstairs to show Dougie something,' said Nigel as he placed the tray with the teapot and cups onto the coffee table in the centre of the room.

'Would you like a biscuit and some squash?' all three kids shook their heads.

Upstairs in Nigel's bedroom, Dougie pulled a brown paper bag he'd hidden from under his jumper. 'Take a look at these,' he said excitedly, pulling some magazines out.

Nigel quickly flicked through the pages and put them under the mattress on his bed. He pressed a five pound note into Dougie's hand. 'Right. Next weekend we're back in business,' he said quietly. 'I'll call you in the week and sort out the details.' Dougie knew what he meant and smiled and nodded.

'Everything all right Mum?' asked Nigel as he and Dougie came back into the room.

'Yes,' she said, 'I've just been telling them all about the flat and how them dirty gypsies won't get out of our bungalow.'

'More tea Douglas?' asked Nigel.

'No we had better be off. I've promised the kids I'd take them to the fun fair.'

'Did you?' asked Dougie's wife.

'Yes, I told you on the way down it was only a quick visit.' He bent down to kiss his Nan and made each of the children do the same, each one of them wiping their mouths with the back of their hands as they moved away. Their gran waved them off. 'It's good to see you,' she said. Nigel gave her a look as if to say 'how two-faced can you get?'

'I'll walk them down to the car. I've got my key and I'll let myself back in,' said Nigel as he shut the front door behind him.

Since Nigel had come home from prison he had sworn to his mum he would have nothing to do with child porn again, but she had her doubts. She wheeled herself to the bottom of the stairs and leant forward out of the chair. She grabbed hold of the banisters and pulled herself up one step at a time. She had no feeling below her waist yet her upper-body strength was amazing. She stopped for breath and twisted her neck as she looked down. She was determined to get to the top, and crawl to her son's bedroom and find out what he did for hours on end in there. He always protested his innocence and that he was merely reading a bible or watching his television. Douglas turning up had made her mind up. Those two sneaky little bastards were up to something and she was going to find the evidence, and with Nigel out of the way, now was as good a time as any. She reached the top of the stairs and propped herself up against his bedroom door. She smiled as she looked back down at the flight of stairs she'd just come up. She was well pleased with herself. The only time she had been up here was when Nigel had lifted her up and carried her to the bathroom which was up here. She usually slept on the sofa in the front room and had never got up here under her own steam. She pulled herself up using the top post of the banisters and held on. Then she pulled the door handle down and opened Nigel's bedroom door. As it swung open she fell inside in a crumpled heap. She was breathing very heavily as she sat up and looked around the untidy room. There was a package on his unmade bed. She moved towards it but suddenly she heard the key go in the lock on the front door. The door opened and then slammed shut.

'Mum?' she heard Nigel shout as he moved from room to room calling her and then the sound of footsteps as he came running up the stairs. 'Mum, what are you doing up here, you could have fallen and hurt yourself.'

'Nigel,' she said looking up at him, 'I want the truth.' Nigel slumped down on the bed and put his head in his hands and cried. She pulled herself up next to him and put her arm around his shoulders. There was floods of tears as he cried like a baby.

'I'm sorry, I'm sorry – I didn't mean to hurt you,' he said. As his mother cuddled him even tighter, he suddenly felt wanted. He hadn't felt such closeness and love and warmth since he was a child. Mum held him for ages and wiped the tears from his cheeks.

'It'll be all right,' she said. 'You can make us a nice cup of tea.' And then for a second she thought about what she'd just said and smiled. 'That is, once you've lifted me back down all those stairs!'

They looked at one another and laughed.

NINE

WHERE DID IT ALL GO WRONG?

Giles walked into the hallway of his flat and hung up his coat. 'It's bloody cold out there,' he said. His wife Annabelle sat at the kitchen table, dabbing at her red eyes and cheeks with a tissue. 'Darling, whatever is the matter?' he asked as he sat down opposite her and clasped her hands in his. He leant forward and kissed her on the cheek. 'Tea?' he asked, standing and picking up two china cups from the draining board. She nodded and smiled as he filled the kettle up and lit the gas. 'Where are the children?' he asked.

'They're both playing outside in the field with their friends,' she said. 'I'm sorry, but I just can't get used to living here. I seem to be having one of those terrible off days. I'm at my wits' end and feel like ending it all. It's the children I feel sorry for, they have nowhere to play in this rabbit-hutch, we have no back garden and I know they've made some new friends here but they miss their old friends terribly.'

Giles put his arm around his wife's waist as she stood up and they held onto one another. 'It's all my fault. If only I hadn't been so damned stupid,' he said, seeming to slip into a trance, staring straight ahead. His wife was talking to him, but in his dream state he couldn't hear what she was saying. He had been to see his doctor about these funny turns which seemed to hit him every now and then, but the doctor put it down to a form of shock, or a sort of anxiety attack. He broke out into a cold sweat and his stomach tightened. 'I'd better go and get the children,' he said, looking at his watch, 'the first show starts in half an hour.'

Giles was taking his two children to see the circus that had been set up on the playing field in the middle of the estate. It had been there for a week, and that evening was its last night before it moved off to a neighbouring town. The children were so excited about going. They were fascinated by the huge, candy-striped canvas big top, surrounded by the helpers' and performers' caravans, in the centre of the field. Inside the circle of mobile homes were the cages which housed the performing animals, and it wasn't often that the roar of a lion could be heard in deepest, darkest South London. Lots of their friends from school had been, so Giles had decided to give them a treat, even though money was a bit tight. 'Are you sure you won't join us?' he asked.

'No,' Annabelle said, shaking her head, 'you and the girls go. I'll be all right, I've some sewing to do on my machine and I've got to make up their packed lunches for school in the morning.' Giles kissed his wife and told her he loved her, then went off to find the girls.

'Where's Mum?' they asked when Giles found them whizzing down the slide in the children's playground.

'She's not feeling too good, so she's having a lie down.'

'Does that mean she isn't coming with us?'

He shook his head. He knew it wasn't worth lying to the

girls. They had both seen their mother upset and in tears so often over the last few months. 'Mum said that us three should go and enjoy ourselves and that she'd wait up and you can tell her all about the circus when we get in.'

They joined the queue which snaked across the worn grass from the tiny box office where they watched an elderly woman beaver away dishing out the tickets. As they got near the front, through a gap in the caravans they saw a clown putting the finishing touches to his make up, a cowboy practising lassoing a thick heavy rope around a wooden post and a man running a pair of zebras up and down. They stood there open-mouthed, trying to take it all in.

The family's lives had been turned upside-down over the past year. They had once lived in a large five-bedroomed house in a fashionable area. They had had their own swimming pool and tennis courts, and a gardener had come three times a week to cut the grass and tend the gardens. They had also had a cleaner that came in every day and a live-in French au pair girl who took care of the children and babysat whilst Giles and Annabelle went out to dinner parties, the opera or the theatre, as they did most evenings. This lavish lifestyle had come to an abrupt end when one evening disaster had struck and their lives had changed forever.

'Are you ready darling?'

'Yes, yes, I'm just finishing my make-up.'

'Do hurry, Bill has brought the car round to the front.'

Bill was normally employed as Giles and Annabelle's gardener, but tonight he would be driving their prized Bentley convertible to a Summer Ball which the company Giles worked for in the City was throwing. Giles worked in the futures market and had been with the company since joining them straight from university. He had worked his way up and was now a senior partner in the firm. He had been headhunted by other companies, but had stayed loyal and was rewarded with wage increases and large bonuses, hence the Bentley.

Waiting for the car outside, he nervously fiddled with the button on his dinner suit and checked his black bow tie in the mirror as the Bentley pulled up at the front of the house. His wife appeared at the front door and came down the steps and onto the gravel drive. She turned and waved to her daughters, who were with the au pair, waving from their bedroom window. Giles opened the back door and his wife slid across the beige leather upholstery. He lowered himself in beside her. 'You look beautiful tonight darling,' he said, squeezing her hand and kissing her on the cheek.

'Would you prefer to have the hood up or down sir?' asked Bill, remembering to put his chauffeur's hat on.

'Down please, William. I'd like everyone to see that the Partridge-Jones' are going out on the town tonight.' The electric hood began to slide back as they drove through the busy streets.

'I booked a holiday today darling,' said Annabelle. 'You've been working so hard recently and I thought it would be nice for you, me and the children to have a few weeks' break in the Caribbean next month.'

'Thank you darling,' said Giles. ' I just hope it doesn't clash with my week's golfing holiday in Portugal with the chaps from the office.'

'No darling, I checked your diary. You're completely free during the two weeks I've booked, but I have had to cancel my long weekend at the health farm with the girls from the bridge club, because it fell directly in the middle of the time we'll be away.'

Giles lit up a cigar as they pulled up outside the hotel where tonight's function was being held. The car came to a halt and Bill jumped out and opened the door for his boss. 'Thank you William, that will be all.' Bill smiled. He knew Mr Partridge-Jones loved all the razzmatazz on nights like these. It gave him a chance to show off his wealth. He was a good man at heart and during the ten years he had worked for him, they had never had a cross word. Giles and his wife had even taken Bill's youngest daughter on holiday to Spain with them one summer. At Christmas Giles would give Bill an envelope with twenty pounds in it, and there was always a present each for Bill's kids, a bottle of whisky for Bill, a turkey and a little something for his wife. He was a generous man who was well liked locally; he would often make generous donations to charities and was always glad to help out at fêtes and garden parties. He loved his wife and his family, and although he was wealthy and a bit of a show-off, he wasn't a big-head.

Giles put his arm around his wife's waist and guided her through the front doors of the hotel, her long sequinned ball gown dragging along the floor. The master of ceremonies, splendid in his red topcoat, which was adorned with a decoration of military medals that dangled from his chest, heralded their arrival. 'Mr and Mrs Partridge-Jones.' Guests stood around chatting and the Partridge-Jones' smiled at a few familiar faces as they entered. They took a glass of champagne offered to them from a silver tray. 'Good to see you old boy,' said Mr Steinberg, the company accountant, 'and may I say, Mrs Partridge-Jones, you're looking as ravishing as ever.' Annabelle smiled and thanked him.

'Don't listen to him Annabelle, he's just an old flirt.'

'Not so much of the old,' said Mr Steinberg as he winked at Annabelle. They stood around, sipping champagne and chatting. It was always nice to meet up with some old faces. A lot of business would be done tonight with some very influential people, from the Government and important companies.

'My Lords, Ladies and Gentlemen, would you please make your way through to the hall and be seated for this evening's dinner.' Giles and Annabelle filed into the hall and looked at the seating plan to find their names. The tables were beautifully laid, with the finest china and cutlery. To Giles's surprise, he was sitting next to Sir Richard Tilbury and his wife Susan. Sir Richard was the Managing Director of the company and was already sitting down, as Giles and Annabelle approached he stood up and shook Giles's hand. Giles introduced his wife Annabelle and Sir Richard introduced his wife to them both. This was the first time they had met socially, although they had seen one another on occasion in the office. Sir Richard was not one to socialise outside work. Giles couldn't believe his luck to be seated next to one of the most powerful men in the city. He would be the envy of everyone he worked with, rubbing shoulders with Sir Richard and the lovely Lady Tilbury, and as he looked around he could see he was already getting some envious looks from the other tables. He smiled back at the sea of faces. 'Jealous bastards,' he thought. 'Look at them, they can't stand it because I'm sitting here.' It made him wonder if Sir Richard had specifically requested that he be seated at his table. Maybe he had heard how well he had done in the previous year, when he'd made huge profits for the company. One thing he did know was that this night would live in his memory forever and he was going to milk it. The tossers in the office wouldn't hear the last of it. He could see their faces when he went back to work – they'd be hanging on his every word as they stood around the coffee machine. 'They won't believe it when I tell them how Sir Richard personally invited my family to his yacht for a month's holiday sailing around the Med,' Giles thought.

He looked at Annabelle, who was deep in conversation with Lady Tilbury. They seemed to be getting on like a house on fire. They were laughing and joking, and chatting about children, schools, shopping at Harrods and horse riding. The champagne was flowing and Giles was knocking it back. Sir Richard seemed to be genuinely interested in Giles's upbringing. It transpired that their fathers had served in the same regiment in the army and had both attended officers' training college at Sandhurst.

After dinner, the men were invited to retire into a side room for a glass of brandy and cigars and Giles was introduced to many people he could have only ever have dreamt about meeting before. Not just money-men, but ambassadors, Lords and MPs had all crowded into the room, which quickly filled with cigar smoke that hung on the ceiling like a cloud.

'My Lords, Ladies and Gentlemen, would you please make your way into the ballroom where this evening's entertainment is about to commence.' The curtain separating the dining area and the ballroom slid back and the band, up on the stage, sprang into life as balloons and streamers fell down from above. Everyone rushed in like young children released from their classrooms at playtime.

The dance floor filled and everyone was having a wonderful time. Giles made sure he had a seat next to Sir Richard, and he listened intently as he chatted to a steady stream of people who came to shake his hand and enquire after his health. After a while Giles became bored with all the bullshit and watched as groups of young lads with more money than sense got louder and louder. They were becoming a bit of a nuisance. One of them picked a girl up and lifted her above his head. The girl screamed as she struggled to keep her dress from lifting up and displaying her underwear to all and sundry. Giles noticed that every so often, one or two of the lads would nip off to the toilets together.

Instead of watching Sir Richard, he now became engrossed with what these lads were up to. He decided to investigate further and so went to the bar and ordered a drink, making sure he stood within earshot of the group. He noticed that when they returned from the toilet they seemed to be full of energy. Perhaps they were on the old wacky-baccy? No, he remembered that when he had tried it at university, all it had done was make him mellow. His speech had become slurred and he'd acted a bit silly for a while, and eventually had fallen asleep. These fella's eyes were bulging out of their heads and they were swinging the girls around like lunatics on the dance floor. He noticed when any of them came back from the toilets they were constantly rubbing their noses and sniffing. Perhaps they had hay fever? He watched and listened and saw one of them handing another something in a paper wrap. A couple of them disappeared in the direction of the toilets. Giles's curiosity got the better of him and he decided to investigate further. The champagne and brandy had given him a couldn't-care-less attitude, and if he could catch these in the act he was sure he would be looked upon as a hero, the man who rid the city of drugs. He could see himself at a ceremony accepting an award from the Commissioner of Police, with Sir Richard shaking his hand and thanking him for his bravery.

Giles kept his distance as he ducked in and out of the people on the dance floor, heading towards the toilets. The two men he'd been following were standing at the urinals. Another man had just finished drying his hands and walked out. A few other people came and went. They looked at Giles suspiciously. Perhaps they had seen him watching them? A cubicle became available and whilst one of the men washed his hands, the other went inside and shut the door. Giles waited for the cubicle next to the man to become free and went inside, stood on the toilet and peered over the top. He could see that the man had sprinkled some white powder into two thin lines about two inches long and was rolling a twenty pound note into a tight funnel. Then, as Giles watched, he bent down and held a finger to one nostril while sniffing the powder up the other, using the note. 'Got you!' shouted Giles. The man looked up and, his face filled with horror, ran from the cubicle and looked around for his friend, who had already left.

Giles, well pleased with himself, climbed down off the toilet and went into the cubicle next door. 'Disgusting habit, I've just caught those two at it,' he said to a man standing at the urinals. He shut the toilet door and dabbed his little finger into the white powder, put it into his mouth and touched it onto his tongue. He was curious to see what it tasted of – nothing in particular. He bent over to smell it.

'Stay right where you are!' said a voice from behind and the unlocked toilet door was abruptly pushed open. Standing there was the hotel security and Sir Richard himself. 'Take him away and call the police,' said Sir Richard, 'we've caught him red-handed.' Giles loudly protested his innocence. 'Ask that man there!' he said, pointing to the man who'd seen it all happen. But he just shrugged his shoulders and walked out.

'Wait, wait,' shouted Giles, 'please tell them what you saw.' It was no good. The man took no notice and disappeared into the crowds.

'We've had reports of three men acting suspiciously,' said the security guard, 'and it looks like we've caught one of them.' Giles was led into an office, where the door was locked behind him as the hotel security waited for the arrival of the police.

Later, at the station, he was charged with possessing cocaine. He was dismissed from his job immediately. A couple of months later he appeared in court and received a three-year suspended sentence. The judge had taken into consideration that he'd never been in trouble with the law before.

With no job, and with the high costs of his defence lawyer, who'd given him bad advice, his savings dwindled rapidly and it wasn't long before his house and his car were repossessed and he had lost nearly everything. No more expensive cars or holidays abroad, or private schooling for the children. The gardener and the au pair both sadly went and the family were homeless and put into a hostel run by the local authority. After a year they were given the flat they were now living in on the estate. Giles's family had all but turned their backs on him, and their so-called friends had stopped calling. They were no longer invited to lavish dinner parties or days out in the country with the horse-riding set. He was stripped of his captaincy at the golf club, where everyone shunned him. Before long he was signing on the dole and the only money coming in besides that was his wife's income from her job as a part-time receptionist at the doctor's surgery. Her family, on the other hand, had been very supportive and helped them out financially whenever they could.

Giles was determined to prove his innocence and, with the help and love of his loyal wife, he knew that one day he would. If only he could find the vital witness from that night at the ball.

TEN

FIX MY CAR

The black-and-white chequered flag waved up and down as Mick crossed the finishing line in first place. He raised a clenched fist in a victory salute in the direction of the stand where his wife and two children were sitting. It had been a good night for him, three races and three wins. Mick did a lap of honour, waved to the crowd and pulled off the track and into the pits. There waiting for him were his jubilant wife and children, who were jumping up and down with excitement. 'Well done love,' said his wife, throwing her arms around his neck and kissing him as he stepped from the car. The children's faces were beaming. Mick pulled his crash helmet off and bent down and kissed and cuddled both of them before wiping the dirt and sweat from his face, using the sleeve of the white boiler suit he wore to race in.

The PA system crackled into life and announced that Mick had been voted the best driver of the night. He stepped back out onto the track, took a bow and waved to the crowd once more, and then received a magnum of champagne and a kiss from a skimpily dressed dolly bird. The important thing was that he was through to the regional finals to be held in a month's time. It had been a lifelong ambition for Mick to get into the finals of the British Banger Racing Championships. Before he left the stadium, he phoned his mum and dad and told them the good news. They were so pleased for him.

Ever since he was a young lad Mick had been car mad. While other kids his age played football out in the street or cricket in the park, Mick had his head under the bonnet of a car. He'd spend hours stripping down old cars and rebuilding them, and by the time he was fourteen he was repairing his neighbours' cars for them. As a teenager he'd got into a spot of bother with the law as they caught him trying to steal a motor. He had escaped prison by the skin of his teeth; his dad's friend, who owned a garage, had gone to court with him and spoken up on his behalf. He had told the judge that the boy wasn't a bad kid and had even said that to help him keep out of trouble when he left school the next month, he would be more than willing to take him on as an apprentice mechanic. The magistrate had thought long and hard and took into account the fact that Mick had no previous convictions. He bound Mick over to keep the peace for two years and told him in no uncertain terms that if he ever came before him again, he would end up in prison.

Since that day Mick had never looked back. He finished his apprenticeship at his dad's mate's garage, and ended up working for himself later. When he was seventeen Mick took his driving test and passed the first time. He and his workmate Jeff bought an old banger which they intended to do up and use for getting to and from work, but when they got it home, they realised that it was going to cost them a small fortune to get it roadworthy. Mick had the bright idea to strip it down, take all the glass out of the windows, modify the engine slightly and use it for stock car or banger racing, which they did. That old car got them onto the first rung of the ladder and into the world of racing. As Mick had a driver's licence and Jeff didn't, Mick was the driver and Jeff the mechanic. They had lots of fun with that old car and soon became hooked on the sport.

Mick's win tonight was the pinnacle of his driving career and on the drive home to the estate, memories of those early days came flooding back. 'I bet old Jeff would be over the moon if he knew I had got into the regional finals.' Jeff had emigrated to Australia about five years before. He had married not long after completing his apprenticeship and he and his wife, with their newborn baby, had decided to look for work on the other side of the world. They had kept in touch for a couple of years, with Mick promising to visit his friend, but the only communication they had now was a Christmas card every year.

'Why don't you give him a ring,' suggested Mick's wife. 'He'd be well pleased to hear from you.'

Mick looked at his watch. 'Well, if it's half ten here, what would the time be in Sydney?'

'Aren't they ten hours in front?' asked his wife.

'No, I think you'll find they're eight hours behind, aren't they?' said Mick, laughing, unable to work it out. 'I'll phone him one day, whatever the time difference.'

'Make sure you do,' said his wife, 'he'd be so happy to hear about your win.'

Mick backed the trailer carrying his banger racer onto the parking space outside his ground-floor flat and threw the champagne he'd won onto the back seat. Out of the dozen cars parked there, eight of them either belonged to him or to clients he was repairing them for. If anyone on the estate had a problem with their car they came to Mick. The problem was that being such a nice guy, and so easygoing, Mick didn't charge what he should for some jobs. If any elderly person came to him he would do their work and tell them when they asked how much it was that he hadn't worked the cost out yet, or else he'd say, 'Get us a pint when you see me over in the pub next.' His wife always said that he was far too soft, and that the money he had failed to collect could have bought them a mansion.

The next day Mick was up bright and early. He tried ringing Jeff out in Aussie, but the international operator told him that all the lines were busy. He looked out of the kitchen window as he slipped on his blue, grease-covered overalls, buttoned them up to his waist and sat down to pull on his black slip-on Chelsea boots. 'I think it's trying to rain,' he said.

'Mmm,' replied his wife noncommittally, knowing that Mick didn't need much of an excuse not to work. 'Don't forget to bring in that bottle of champagne you won last night.'

'Yeah, I will in a minute.' Mick grabbed his toolbox from the hallway, thinking he'd better make a start, when the phone rang. He picked it up. 'Yeah, yeah, that's no problem, if you can't get it over to me I'll come round to you and take a look at it. Yeah, yeah, I'll see you soon.' Mick put his arms around his wife's waist as she stood at the kitchen sink. 'That was Dave from the pub, his sister is staying with him and she's having trouble with her car. Put the kettle on love, I'll have another cuppa before I drive round there.'

She said nothing.

'Did you hear what I said? That was Dave on the phone.'

'Yes, yes, I heard.' She dried her hands on the tea towel hanging from the cooker and walked across the kitchen and flicked the kettle on. Mick sat back down and began to flick through the morning paper he had left on the kitchen table. A cup of tea was placed in front of him. 'Mick, once you've done this car can we start to get rid of some of the others we seem to have collected?' Mick thought carefully before he answered.

His wife had a point. Only a few months ago some of the non-drivers amongst the tenants had signed a complaint about Mick and his cars, and as a result a council official had paid Mick a visit. He had wanted to know if it was true, as stated in the letter signed by the tenants, that Mick was actually running a business from his home address. Mick, however, had been one step ahead. He'd heard a rumour that he was due a visit and had removed most of the cars he had been working on, spreading the others around the estate. He had even parked three or four outside the pub, but left the battered white Cortina he used for racing on the trailer outside his flat. For some reason the official never noticed that. Perhaps he was a fan?

In the car park there were large patches of oil here and there and the man became quite inquisitive, to say the least, as to where it had come from. Mick just acted dumb and said nothing. There was not enough proof to take the matter any further, but the official suggested that he considered other people in future, when leaving any cars in and around the car park. Mick thanked him for his time and even offered him a cup of tea. 'No, I must be off,' he replied as he got into his own car. He pulled his seatbelt round his ample waist and across his chest and turned the key in the ignition. Nothing happened – the car was as dead as a dodo. The red-faced official unclipped himself and stepped out of the car. 'I don't suppose you can help, can you?' Mick gave him a jump-start and never heard from the council again.

Mick dropped his wife off at the shops and headed round to Dave's, where he and his sister were waiting outside with the bonnet of her car up. Within half an hour Mick had traced the problem to a loose wire hanging from the battery terminals. Mick's wife came over as he cleaned his hands on a piece of old rag.

'All done?' she asked.

'Looks like it,' said Mick.

'How much do I owe you?' asked Dave, pulling some notes from his wallet. Mick looked at his wife. Dave was expecting the usual 'buy me a pint later' routine.

'Two pounds OK?' smiled Mick. Dave handed the money over and Mick handed it to his wife, who looked pleased at his new-found business sense. As they left Dave's place, his wife encouraged him, telling him he should do any future business the same way. 'Do the job and get the cash. It's as easy as that,' she said.

Mick was in the mood now and decided to get cracking on his next job. He had to get an MOT on Mrs Brown's old Morris Minor. He'd had it over a week and hadn't done a thing to it yet. She had been around to his place a couple of times and he'd told her he was waiting for some parts to be delivered. This week he had been more interested in getting his racing car up to scratch, and had had no enthusiasm for work. But once he got started, it only took a couple of hours for him to check over Mrs Brown's car, adjust her brakes and align her front lights, as well as sort out a couple of other minor things. It sailed through the MOT and he delivered the car round to her home. Mick charged her ten pounds and she was well pleased.

'That garage in town charged me fifty pounds last year,' she said as she handed Mick over a crisp ten pound note.

'Cheers Mrs Brown,' he said as he stuffed the note into the top pocket of his boiler suit, both parties more than pleased. He had earned more in wages that day than he had in the last fortnight.

Back home his wife was busy putting the shopping away. 'I'll put the shopping away, you sit down and I'll make us both a nice brew,' Mick told her.

'What's come over you? Why are you acting so nice all of a sudden?' she asked.

'Nothing.' Mick poured the boiling water from the kettle into the teapot. He gave it a quick stir and poured out two cups. Taking a sip, he leant across and held his wife's hand. 'I've been thinking.'

'About what?'

'Well, you know the other night when I tried to get through to Jeff in Australia?'

'Yes.'

'When you went to bed I sat down and wrote a long letter to him, and posted it the next morning.'

'And?' she said.

'I've been thinking, why don't we apply to go out there?'

'What, for a holiday?'

'No, no, for good.'

'What do you mean, live out there?'

Mick nodded his head.

'I've never really thought about it before,' she said.

'Neither had I,' said Mick 'that was until I started writing that letter to Jeff. Then, the next day when I was laying under Mrs Brown's car on the cold, wet concrete feeling damp and miserable and pissed off, I thought to myself "there's got to be more to life than this".'

'What would you do for work?'

'I've even thought of that,' he said. 'You know that darkie who works on the buses?'

'What darkie?'

'The one that lives in the tower block behind us.'

'Oh yeah.'

'Well, the other week I was servicing his car.'

'I thought he was a mechanic.'

'He was, but he's an inspector now, so I suppose he doesn't want to get his hands dirty. Anyway, if you'd let me finish, he was telling me that at the bus depot where he works, they are always on the lookout for qualified fitters. So I was thinking if I got a job on the buses and worked there for six months they could give me a reference for Australia.'

'How will we afford to get there?'

'We'll do what Jeff done, become ten pound poms.'

'What about our parents and my brothers and your sister and the kids and their friends and the cat and the dog?'

'We won't all be able to go for a tenner!' laughed Mick.

'I don't mean that.'

'I know, I know, I'm only pulling your leg, still, it's worth thinking about, all that sunshine, clear blue skies, deserted beaches, surfing and fishing, barbecues.'

'What's a barbecue?'

'It's like an outside bonfire you cook grub on.'

'Oh,' said she, still none the wiser.

Mick's plan sounded good. The family next door were driving them mad. There were thirteen of them all living in a three-bedroomed house and none of them had done an honest day's work in their lives. They were all claiming benefits and the clothes they wore either came from jumble sales or other people's washing lines. They were the neighbours from hell; why the council had put such a large family under one roof was beyond anyone. It was nothing short of complete madness. Mick had been in the house one night trying to get some spanners he'd lent one of their older boys back, when one of the younger kids returned from the chip shop, where his mum had sent him, carrying a large paper bag. He unwrapped it and tipped the contents onto the threadbare carpet. Chips and saveloys, and a couple of Cornish pasties, were all spread out on the floor. Plates and cutlery were clearly not needed at feeding time in this house. The whole family sat around crosslegged and helped themselves with their fingers, the oldest and biggest members of the clan claiming the extra-big pieces of pasty and saveloy.

Mick was up bright and early the next day with his head under the bonnet, putting the final touches to his pride and joy. Tonight was the grand final and he wanted everything to be just perfect. He listened to the engine purring with satisfaction, but when he revved it up a cloud of black smoke billowed from the exhaust. 'Nothing to worry about,' thought Mick. 'After all, I haven't started her up since the last meeting.' He shut the engine down and checked the oil and water. Everything was fine, there were no leaks. He climbed down from the trailer and went indoors.

His wife had just finished ironing the white all-in-one racing suit which he would be wearing that night. While she went and picked up the kids from school, he popped over to Mr Singh's to get some fags, a bottle of coke and some chewing gum. 'Good luck,' said Mr Singh. 'I hope you do well.' Next stop was the pub, where Dave was busy tidying up after the lunchtime session. He seemed to have the hump for some reason, and wasn't his usual cheery self. There had been plans to run a minibus from the pub to watch the final, but a lot of people who had put their names down had suddenly backed out when Dave had asked for a deposit.

'You there tonight Dave?' asked Mick.

Dave didn't look up from the table he was wiping down. 'I'll try Mick, but the way things are looking here, with the lack of staff, I'll be hard pushed to get there.'

Mick could sense that Dave didn't want to chat. 'Right, I'll be off then.'

'Yeah, good luck,' said Dave as he wiped the inside of an ashtray.

THE ESTATE

Mick headed off home, wondering if the two quid he had charged Dave's sister to get her motor going had given him the hump, or if his old woman and daughter were up to their tricks again.

Back home he sat down for a bite to eat but ended up just pushing the food around the plate; the butterflies in his stomach had dampened his appetite. He lit up a fag and took a long, hard drag. 'Nervous love?' asked his wife.

'A little,' he smiled back at her.

He gathered together everything he needed for the night ahead, his crash helmet, the keys for the race car and his white boiler suit, now hanging from a hanger all neatly pressed. His wife stood up and cuddled him. 'Come on love, let's go and show them what we're made of.' He backed the car up to the trailer, hitched it up and they were off. Some of the neighbours came out and gave them a cheer and a wave as they passed. The kids' faces in the back were a picture. They said they felt like royalty.

As they approached the stadium, the masses of people milling about and queueing to get in slowed the traffic down to a snail's pace. They pulled into the car park and were directed by a steward to the competitors' gate. Mick parked up and reversed the race car from the trailer. It was time to say goodbye to his wife and the kids. 'See ya later champ,' they all said at the same time. They'd obviously been practising his send off.

Mick drove in through the stadium gates and parked up in the pits. Tonight there were to be six heats and the winner of each race would go through to the grand final. Mick lifted the bonnet of the car and gave it one final check. He pulled on his white suit and waited. He had been drawn in heat four, so he had quite a wait before he was out there. After the first race he walked out onto the track and looked around the jam-packed stadium. The atmosphere was electric and the smell of car fumes filled the air. He spotted where the family were seated and gave them a wave and the thumbs up. The kids were so excited and proud of their dad.

Race two was over and Mick was asked by the steward to go and get himself ready, and to listen out for instructions over the tannoy. A voice crackled into life. 'Gentlemen, please listen carefully. Those in heat four please wait until all the cars from heat three have left the track. When they have I will lead you out on foot, so will you please follow slowly behind me in your vehicles and take up your allocated positions for the start of your race.' The cars in Mick's heat began to move slowly from underneath the grandstand. A wall of sound hit them as the crowd's cheers were drowned out by cars revving. The smell of burning fuel and oil mixed with the scent of onions from the hot dog stalls rose into the air.

Everyone got ready as the starter looked along the line. He raised his flag above his head and dropped it. Dust and smoke swirled around. They were off! Well, the others were. Mick had begun to pull away, but his engine had stalled. The rest of the cars were well away to the sound of roaring engines, leaving Mick behind. He turned the key and the engine came to life. He put his foot flat on the accelerator and the car chugged forward at a top speed of 5 mph. In frustration Mike banged the steering wheel with his clenched fists and he called the car all the names under the sun.

He managed to get the car off the track before the engine cut out again, and limped back into the pits with the help of a handful of race marshals pushing him. The crowd outside cheered home the winner of the race. 'Just my fucking luck,' said Mick shaking his head in disbelief. He pulled his helmet off and slung it onto the back seat. He held his head in his hands and felt like crying. 'Fuck it, fuck it, fuck it!' he repeated. Then he heard a voice he recognised and looked up. Standing in front of him was his family. 'Don't worry Dad,' said his little girl. 'We still love you.'

Mick bent down, pulled all three of them together and held them tightly. 'I'm sorry, I let you down,' he said with tears in his eyes.

'There's always next year,' said his wife.

Mick held her hand and looked her in the eyes. 'We won't be here next year love, we'll be playing with the kids on a beach Down Under.'

She smiled. 'Well, what are you waiting for? You'd better give Jeff a call then when we get home.'

ELEVEN

GRASS

'What do ya reckon then?' The man pulled the roll-up cigarette to his lips and inhaled deeply. He blew out a huge ring of smoke and in between coughing and gagging managed to say, 'Yeah man, that's good gear. Wrap me up an ounce.'

'I told you you'd like it man,' said Pete, grinning as he cut into the nine-inch long bar of Paki Black. He picked up the piece he'd hacked off and placed it on the weighing scales. 'There you go man, it's just over the ounce, so you've got yourself a good deal.'

'Nice one,' he said, passing the joint in his hand over to Pete. 'Get the last lug out of that.' The man handed over his money to Pete and shook his hand. Pete showed him to the front door, poked his head out and looked along the balcony. 'Right, it's all clear, see ya later.' He slapped the man on the back and watched him making his way towards the lifts.

Pete went inside and pulled the bolts on the top and bottom of the door across. His girlfriend Lucy came out of the bathroom with her hair wrapped in a towel. 'How'd it go?' she asked, drying her hair as she spoke.

'Yeah, fine. I think we have another satisfied customer, who'll probably be back.'

'Good,' she said, walking into the bedroom, taking off her dressing-gown and picking up the underwear she'd laid out on the bed. Pete looked at her. 'Don't bother putting that on, I've got plans for you.' He walked towards her and pushed her backwards onto the bed.

Pete and Lucy lived on the top floor of one of the tower blocks, but they were not staying there with the council's blessing, they were squatting. Lucy's brother Phil had been one of the painters and decorators who'd worked on the flats when they were being built, and the flat they were now squatting in was once used by the decorators as a temporary storeroom where they had kept their equipment. Phil had gone to the locksmiths in town and had a duplicate key cut, and when the block was completed he'd handed the original key back in to the site agent, then given Lucy his key. When other people had started to move in to the estate, Pete and Lucy had moved their gear into the flat and changed the locks. They had been living there for a couple of months now, but it had taken the council a few weeks to cotton on to the fact that they were squatting.

The flat was obviously set aside for another family, who were unable to gain entry, so the council had to put them into a hotel and their furniture into storage while they took Pete and Lucy to court to get them out. The bailiffs had tried to force entry, but had beaten a hasty retreat when one of Pete's pet Dobermans had leapt up and tried to take a chunk out of one of them as he lowered his arse in backwards through the kitchen window. Numerous letters had arrived with dates to go to court, but Pete had just ripped them up and thrown them in the bin. The police, responding to complaints from other residents, had also been around a couple of times, but they too had failed to gain entry or get any answer. The problem was that with the flat being on the top floor, right at the end of the landing, anyone coming to the flat could be heard before they got there. Plus, Pete had a big mirror fixed to the wall at an angle. He could sit in the kitchen and see if anybody was approaching, which gave Pete and Lucy plenty of warning to batten down the hatches. Pete knew it was only a matter of time before he got busted by the old bill or evicted by the council. He was not long out of prison, where he had done a three-year sentence for selling hashish. Lucy was one of his regular customers in a pub he used to sell from.

Since he came out and moved onto the estate, he had built up a regular clientele. People would come and go at all hours of the day and night. Music would be blaring and there'd be shouting, screaming and laughing. Business was booming, one reason being the tabloid press and music papers had just run a big story on a festival in the States. There had been reports of kids dancing trance-like, naked and on drugs, with flowers in their hair, singing of peace and love. Naturally, British kids, curious about what was happening on the other side of the Atlantic, wanted to jump on the bandwagon and emulate their American cousins by trying out some of these fashionable drugs.

News of any supplies arriving at Pete's place soon spread. All types of people came to buy, not just the drop-out hippie types. Drugs had progressed and there was a new market. At one time beatniks and hippies were the only ones indulging, but now drugs had crossed into the mainstream. Doctors, nurses, bus drivers, builders, road sweepers, people from all walks of life were using them. Pete sold all types of hash: Red Lebanese, Paki Black, Moroccan, grass and weed, in different quantities, from enough to make up one spliff, up to a dozen ounces. Pills were another good seller. He'd get through hundreds of pills a week. LSD and speed were some of his best sellers, while cocaine and heroin were bought mainly by his more professional clients. Pete had tried every drug there was to try, but he and Lucy liked nothing more than to chase the dragon, something they did most days. They would often sit with customers and have a few bottles of beer, listen to some loud, headbanging music and smoke heroin.

Pete used to belong to a well-known motorbike gang and had once been involved in a fight with a rival gang. A man had been shot and wounded and another hit by an axe, losing part of an ear. The trouble had started over an argument in a pub car park about payment for a drugs deal. Pete and his mates had double-crossed the other gang by stealing the drugs they were selling and robbing them at gunpoint of all the money they had on them. They thought they had got away with it because they had put about 30 miles between the other gang and themselves. Feeling they were safe, they decided to pull into a petrol station to fill up and buy some fags. The attendant had noticed the handgun Pete was carrying as he unzipped his leather jacket and took some money out. One of the other boys with them was also losing a lot of blood from where he had been cut on his arm. Blood was flowing from the sleeve of his slashed leather jacket. Unbeknown to them, the police were called as soon as they left the garage and a roadblock was set up. When they turned the corner in a quiet country lane they saw a policeman in a fluorescent jacket standing in the middle of the road, waving and shining a torch as he flagged them down. They did a quick U-turn and headed back the way they had come, but as they turned, a line of police cars with blue flashing lights blocked them in. Pete and a couple of others headed into the woods while the rest of them roared off across the open fields. Pete drove like a madman in the dark forest, weaving in and out of the trees, but his luck ran out when he reached a river and the police blocked him in. The two fellas with him managed to dump their bikes, swim across the river and disappear into the night. Before he was jumped on and arrested he had just enough time to dump the gun into the murky, fast-flowing waters.

He was taken down to the police station and put in the cells for the night. It wasn't long before the police put two and two together and connected Pete with the shooting that had taken place earlier that evening. A man with gunshot wounds was fighting for his life in hospital, while another, with part of his ear missing, was in the hospital operating theatre as they spoke. Although Pete knew that the rival gang would not speak about what had happened if they were arrested, he was worried that the police would somehow gather enough evidence to put him away for a long time. A senior officer told him that it was only a matter of time before they found the gun that was used, and then they would have all the evidence they needed to charge him with attempted murder, or murder if either of the two men died. 'You're looking at doing a lot of bird my old son,' said the copper. 'We can make it so much easier for you. We know you weren't alone, just tell us a few names and we can sort something out. There's certain people you know that we'd love to have a chat with.'

Sitting in the drab, grey-painted cell a hundred things went through Pete's mind. He might never see his girlfriend again, and what would his mum and dad, brothers and sisters think? His dad had always warned him that he was heading for trouble and was mixing with the wrong crowd. There was only one thing for it. Pete stood up and banged on the heavy steel cell door with his fist. 'Open up, I need to speak to someone.' A few minutes later he heard footsteps coming down the corridor and the sound of a bolt being slid back as the door opened. A uniformed policeman stood in front of him. 'I need to speak to a senior copper,' said Pete. The door was slammed shut in his face and locked.

What seemed like hours passed before he again heard movement on the other side, then the door was re-opened and standing there with a couple of other men in suits was the head of CID. He was taken from the cell and walked to an interview room. He sat down at a desk and his solicitor came in and sat beside him. Facing them were two coppers.

'Right, what is it you want to say?' asked one of the coppers as the other scribbled away on a notepad.

'I want to tell you everything,' said Pete, 'not just what happened last night, but everything to do with the boys from the motorcycle club.'

The two coppers smiled at one another and as one carried on writing, the other pulled a packet of cigarettes from his pocket and handed one to Pete. 'Shall I order some tea?' he asked. Things were far more civilised now that Pete had decided to come clean.

Pete was held for another 48 hours before being released on police bail, and in the subsequent weeks the police raided over 200 homes across England and made 150 arrests. Large amounts of drugs and guns were seized and suitcases full of used notes were taken away. It was all over the papers and the head of the investigation appeared on television, saying it was all due to good police work that these people had been apprehended and their gangs disbanded.

Pete was never charged with the shooting or any other offence, but to his former friends, he was a marked man and there was a price on his head. For a time he lived and worked in Ireland and would come back to England to visit his family every now and then. After a couple of years he moved out to France, where he stayed before moving down to southern Spain. It was there that he met a Moroccan man who got him into the world of drug dealing. The rewards were high and in no time at all he had made himself some serious money.

Having made his contacts, he returned to England and set up a business of his own. All had gone well; he had even managed to buy his own house outright with cash, he drove a brand new American Cadillac and his suits were sharp and made to measure, like his shoes and shirts. Business was booming. That was until he got careless one evening and sold some blow to an undercover copper. The following night the pub was raided and he was caught in possession and hauled off to the cells. This time there was no bargaining. He was remanded in custody and six months later was sentenced to three years for dealing in cannabis and amphetamines.

The first night inside he was queueing for food when he noticed that the con dishing up the food was one of his former motorbike mates. The bloke looked at him and never said a word as he slapped the runny potato and burnt-to-a-cinder meat onto his plastic tray, 'Cheers mate,' said Pete nervously. Before he could walk away the bloke coughed up a greenie from deep in his throat and spat it into his food. He nodded at the man and offered him his hand 'No hard feelings, eh?' The bloke stared back, not acknowledging his feeble greeting. That night before lights out and lock-up he was lying on his bunk staring at the ceiling when two men appeared in the doorway of his cell. One of them threw a piece of rope tied in a hangman's noose onto the bed. 'Do it yourself or we'll do it for you,' he said, and they walked away laughing. He was unable to sleep that night. The bloke in the bed below didn't help, he snored like a pig all night and the bunk bed squeaked as he fidgeted and shouted and talked in his sleep.

At seven o'clock the next morning the cell door was unlocked and he went along to the toilets with all the other cons to slop out his bucket and fill up his plastic water jug. He remembered emptying the bucket and someone saying 'fancy meeting you here', then he felt a burning sensation down his neck and back. Fresh air seemed to flow into the back of his newly open, vented shirt. He then felt unbelievable pain as dampness spread down his back and into his pants. He was left standing all alone as those around him quickly moved out of his way and made themselves scarce. When he looked down he could see a puddle of crimson blood forming around his feet. He knew then he had been slashed with a razor from his neck down to his buttocks. His head spun as he collapsed into a heap on the floor. He remembered calling out for help, and someone leaning over him saying 'die you cunt'. The next thing he recalled was coming around in the local hospital with a prison officer sitting at the end of his bed. By all accounts he had lost a lot of blood and was lucky to still be alive.

After his stay in hospital he was returned to prison, where he spent the rest of his sentence going between the prison hospital and the segregation wing. On his release, the governor mentioned the incident and said he hoped Pete had learnt a lesson. He remarked that those who live by the sword, die by the sword. Outside the prison gates Lucy was waiting for him with a kiss and a nice big spliff, and the keys to their new flat on the estate. A few weeks later they moved in and he was back dealing.

One day Andy, a mate of his, came to the flat and told Pete he was off to Holland the next day to buy some good quality gear. He asked if Pete wanted to come along and make himself a few quid, explaining that he was making the trip with a lorry driver friend of his, who was taking a delivery of cigarettes out to the Dutch capital. 'We can go across as foot passengers and meet him in the nearest bar on the other side, and then travel with him in the lorry into Amsterdam. He can go off, unload and do whatever he has to, while we go and buy our gear. We'll meet up with him later, stash the gear in the truck and go back with him to the bar near the port, then make the return journey as foot passengers. Once across, we'll meet up with him again.' Andy pointed out that prices for drugs in Holland were cheaper than in Britain and there was less hassle from the old bill there, so there would be more profit when they got back.

Pete discussed the plan with Lucy. She wasn't too happy about it and they decided they didn't want it to become a regular trip. Lucy felt it was time to get away from the drug scene. 'It's only a matter of time before we get our arses busted by the filth or some rival dealer feels like we're getting too big for our boots and decides to take us out. I've had enough of this life. When you get back from this trip let's both sit down and talk about moving on and starting a new life somewhere else, somewhere no one knows us and we can live our lives in peace. I hate looking over our shoulders all the time and peeping through the spy hole or the curtains every time there's a knock at the front door. I'm tired of waiting for a tap on the shoulder and a copper reading me my rights, and I don't want to carry on telling my sister and my parents lies. For God's sake, they think I work with kids in a nursery school, they'd die if they knew that I lived with a drugs dealer and didn't work for a living. They'd die if they knew where and how I lived my life.' Tears trickled down her cheeks. 'Pete, all I'm saying is this has got to stop, do you hear me?'

Pete nodded. 'Yes, I hear you.'

'Things have got to change. I'm a young woman with my whole life ahead of me, one day I want to get married and have children and live in a nice house, is that too much to ask?'

'I agree with everything you've said, but how am I going to get the money to pay for all those things?'

'Work, Pete, like everyone else has to, get yourself a proper job.'

'Doing what?'

'Anything except dealing!' she shouted. 'You're good with your hands, you've tinkered with motorbikes since you were a kid, why not get yourself a little lockup somewhere and start a bike repair business?'

'OK, OK. When I get back tomorrow night we'll sit down and talk about it, I promise. Now wipe your eyes and when I get back I'll go halves with ya on that baby you're talking about.'

The next morning Pete was up before it was light and set off. The roads out of London and down through Kent were clear, and a couple of hours later they were pulling up outside a transport café in Dover town centre, where the driver dropped them off and headed for the boat. Pete and Andy walked across to the ferry terminal and bought a couple of passenger tickets. Andy could see his mate queueing to get on board. Everything looked hunky-dory. They made their way onto the boat and made no contact with the lorry driver while on board. Once on the other side, they walked into the town and waited in a bar before hopping back into the lorry and driving straight through France and Belgium, eventually arriving in Amsterdam.

Within a few hours they had done their business and had a couple of holdalls loaded up. Back at the rendezvous for the return trip home, they stashed the bags under the drivers' seat and covered them with spare parts and tools. All had gone well and they were soon back on the boat for the channel crossing. They watched and waited until they saw their friend pull out of the ferry and go through customs before they disembarked. They made their way unchecked through the customs hall and walked back to the pub in town where they were meeting the lorry, where they had a couple of pints and jumped into the waiting lorry. The driver checked his wing mirrors to see if they were being followed. 'Well chaps,' he said, 'I think we've done it.' They all cheered and shook hands and cracked open a couple of cans of ale.

It was dark as the lorry pulled in behind Pete's block of flats. Pete had noticed that a car had been following them for the last mile or so, but didn't want to say anything to the other two. He grabbed his bag and climbed out of the lorry. The car stopped. He jumped to the ground. 'It was good to do business with you both.' Pete walked towards his block and waved as the lorry drove past him. Out of the corner of his eye, he noticed two men sitting in a parked car to the right. He recognised one of them as a DCI from the local nick. He looked up towards his flat, where the lights were on. A floor below his he could see what looked like a policeman's helmet looking down from the balcony at him, and out of the shadows stepped a man in a long, dark coat. He had a hat pulled down covering most of his face and was holding something in his hand. What did he do? Pete was caught in two minds. Did he run, or did he stand and see what they had to say?

The sound of a motorbike came roaring up behind him and stopped about six feet away. Its lights were on full beam, blinding Pete as he tried to work out who was riding it. He clutched the holdall to his chest. There was no way they were taking this from him, he'd worked fucking hard getting it. He walked towards the dark figure in front of him. The man lifted what he was holding, which Pete could now see was a gun, and pointed it at him. Pete stared down the long barrel. 'Hello Pete, how you keeping, long time no see.' Then there were three quick bangs and flashes of yellow and blue light. Pete could smell gunpowder and felt a burning pain in his chest and groin. As he slumped to the floor he felt the bag being lifted from him. He could hear a voice as he began to drift off to sleep. 'Cheers Pete, thanks for the gift.'

TWELVE

THE TAVERN ON THE GREEN

Dave poured out a light ale into the half-filled glass of bitter and handed it over the bar. He took the money, counted it, opened the till and dropped the coins into the tray inside. 'Heard any more about the shooting?' asked old Fred, one of the Tavern's regulars.

'No, no, nothing, it's gone a bit quiet,' replied Dave as he picked up some pint glasses and cleaned them with a bar towel. He held one up to the light.

'There's been loads of rumours going around as to who did it.'

Dave smiled. 'There's always rumours going around, especially something like a shooting, and I'll bet you're responsible for half of them.'

Old Fred took a sip of his pint and laughed. 'You cheeky bastard! A few people I've spoken to think the old bill shot him. I did hear that he pulled a gun on them.'

Dave shook his head. 'Rumours, who knows what really happened.'

'Bottle of Guinness please Dave. Hello Fred, how are you?'

'Fine young Michael, how about yourself?'

'Yeah, can't complain.'

Dave poured the bottle into a half-pint glass. 'Did the wife let you out? Or did you run out?' Dave and Fred burst out laughing.

'All right, all right, ain't you overdone the joke?' Mick smiled. A couple of months had passed and he was still getting the piss taken out of him over his appearance in the banger racing finals. Before the event he had gone over the car with a fine-tooth comb and checked everything except, that is, the fuel levels. It wasn't till a few days after having to retire from the meet when his car conked out that he had been able to summon up the enthusiasm to find out what the problem was. Only then did he discover his mistake.

'Funny though, ain't it,' said Dave, looking at Mick, still in fits of giggles.

Dave's wife Wendy appeared in the bar, stuck a glass under the vodka optic and got herself a drink. She poured half a bottle of Slimline tonic in and took a sip. 'That's better,' she said, finishing the rest of the drink in the next mouthful. 'Don't get too used to that,' said Fred.

'Too late, I already have,' she replied as she bent down and stacked some bottles of beer on the cold shelf. Dave looked at her, mumbled something and walked to the other end of the bar. She carried on talking to Fred while she served someone else.

Dave and his wife weren't on particularly good terms at the moment. They'd had a row about their daughter Kerry, who, as all the customers knew, was a right little madam who seemed to love causing trouble. She was eighteen now and although she was paid by Dave and Wendy to work in the pub, she found time to do very little. She was a right lazy cow, and when behind the bar had eyes for most men under the age of 30. Dave could only say so much to her because he wasn't her real father. Wendy had been married before and Dave had come into their lives when Kerry was six years old.

From the first time Kerry and Dave met she had played her mother up. Dave had turned up to take Wendy out on a date, and Kerry had created, crying and screaming and throwing herself on the floor, holding her breath because she didn't want her mum leaving her at home with the babysitter whilst she went out with a man. She cried that it was unfair and she wanted her real dad to come back and live with them. In the end Wendy had had to give in, and she and Dave had spent the evening at home, watching the television with Kerry sitting in between them and refusing to go to bed. Ever since that day the spoilt brat had got her own way.

Kerry was at the heart of most of the rows Dave and Wendy had. This morning, for instance, she was meant to get out of bed early and give her mum and Dave a hand with a special delivery from the brewery. The wagon had turned up and Dave and the deliveryman had got to work unloading the barrels and crates of beer. Meanwhile, Wendy unpacked a load of groceries from the back of her car and put them into the fridge and freezer in the pub's kitchen. 'Kerry!' she shouted up the stairs as she struggled in with another box. There was no answer. 'Kerry, can you come down here and give me a hand please!' Wendy looked at the clock. It was 10 a.m. 'Kerry, will you get your arse down these stairs and give me a hand please.' There was still no movement. An hour passed and a delivery of bread and rolls and cakes turned up from the Italian bakers in town. Dave, having finished in the cellar and washed his hands in the kitchen sink, got to work stacking the bread away in the kitchen.

Wendy meanwhile was hoovering around the carpet in the saloon and public bar areas, having finished mopping out the gents' and ladies' toilets and polishing the tables and the top of the bar. She switched the hoover off and unplugged and wound up the lead.

'I'm done in the kitchen,' said Dave, plonking himself down in the chair and lighting up a well-earned cigarette.

'Did Kerry help you?' asked Wendy, winding the hoover's lead up.

'I thought she was giving you a hand,' replied Dave.

'I'll put the kettle on and you can go up and give her a shout.'

Walking up the stairs, Dave shouted her name. 'Kerry, Kerry, are you up yet?' He heard movement and stopped and listened outside her bedroom door. He could hear voices and giggling. Perhaps she was on the phone to one of her mates. He opened the door slightly and put his head around the door and looked inside. In the near darkness it was hard for him to see anything at first. The curtains were still pulled together, with only a shaft of daylight shining onto one of the walls through the gap in the velvet curtains. He stepped inside the room. 'Kerry, are you all right? Are you awake yet?' Silence. Dave walked across the room and pulled back the curtains. Sunlight streamed into the room. Kerry was lying naked in bed. She looked at him, then sat upright and grabbed the sheet to cover herself with. Lying with his feet on the pillow near her head, and with his head between her legs, was a naked man. He turned himself round and sat up, looked at Kerry and smiled, then looked at Dave and stood up. 'Morning Mr Knight, how are you?'

Dave stared at him, his temper coming to the boil. 'I'll give you good fucking morning!' Dave snatched up some of the clothes that were scattered around the room and threw them at the man. 'Get your gear and fuck off out of my pub,' he said angrily. Kerry slipped on a dressing-gown and laughed nervously as the man, in his rush to get dressed, began stepping into Kerry's white lacy knickers. 'Sorry, sorry,' he said, stepping out of them and putting his own pants on.

'Phone me later,' said Kerry, kissing the man on the cheek as he rushed past Dave and down the stairs, buttoning up his shirt as he went.

'You fucking little tramp!' said Dave as he walked towards Kerry, his fists clenched at his side. She looked at him straight in the eyes. She could tell Dave wanted to hit her. 'Go on, do it, you ain't got the bottle,' she snarled. 'You dare come anywhere near me and I'll tell Mum that you're a dirty pervert, that you've tried to kiss and touch me and that you've begged me to go to bed with you. She ain't going to be too happy, so I suggest you back off.'

Wendy, hearing the commotion, came into the room. 'What's going on?' she demanded, a worried look on her face.

'Ask your precious daughter, she'll tell you,' said Dave as he turned and walked down the stairs. He went into the kitchen, sat down at the table and lit up a cigarette. He could hear raised voices up above. A door slammed and then silence. Wendy came downstairs and stood leaning against the sink. Dave looked over at her; he could tell she'd been crying. Her eyes were red and her mascara had run, leaving thick black lines halfway down her face. 'You know she's blaming you, don't you?'

Dave looked at her in disbelief. 'How do you work that out?'

'She says you're being far too strict, and that you're invading her privacy. All she's doing is rebelling against you and this is her way of telling you that she isn't going to put up with it anymore.'

'Wendy, for God's sake, I've just found her in bed with a naked man!'

'She says they're only friends and he missed his bus home

last night, so she offered to let him stay here. It was all innocent, and then you barged in and caused a scene.'

'I don't believe it,' said Dave. 'Her so-called friend must also be a gynaecologist.'

'There you go again,' replied Wendy.

'Well, his head was halfway up her . . .'

'Dave, I don't want to hear it,' said Wendy, holding her hands up to indicate that she'd heard enough.

So it was that Kerry went off to stay at her friend's house, borrowing twenty pounds from her mum before she went, and leaving Dave and Wendy not speaking. Just over a month before Dave had caught Kerry having sex on the floor of the public bar after closing time. This particular night he had locked up for the night and gone off to bed. He had popped his head around Kerry's bedroom door when he saw her light was still on. She said she was reading a good book and wasn't very tired, Dave had fallen fast asleep as soon as his head had hit the pillow. The next thing he knew, Wendy was leaning over him giving him a shake. 'Dave, I can hear voices coming from somewhere downstairs, do you think we've got burglars?'

He slipped on his dressing-gown, grabbed a heavy-duty torch and tiptoed downstairs. He shone the torch down the stairs and into the cellar. It seemed the voices were coming from the saloon bar, and he went quietly in and switched the lights on. There, bent over the bar with her knickers around her ankles was you-know-who, with a man. She turned on the waterworks and told Dave she was sorry, she was drunk and didn't know what she was doing. She blamed the bloke and said that he had made her do it. 'I only did what you asked me to do,' he said in his defence. Dave threw him out. Kerry begged him not to tell her mum. 'Please, please, it will never happen again.' Dave had kept his word. He had told his wife that the noise she'd heard was Rex, their Jack Russell dog, scratching at the back door to get out. 'He must have heard something in the back yard, a cat or a fox or something, anyway, let's get some kip,' he said as he pulled the blanket back up to his chin and wished his wife a good night's sleep. To that day Wendy did not know what Dave had discovered that night, although it would have been so easy for him to tell his wife that this morning wasn't the first time he had found his stepdaughter in a compromising position with a man.

The following morning the silence between Dave and his missus continued, even though it was a big day for Dave and the pub's football team. It was their cup final day, and they were playing against the team second behind them in the league. It was a local derby and there was a great deal of pride at stake. If they won today and gained one more point from their last three games, then they would have won the league and cup double. Dave had promised all the players at the beginning of the season that if they won the double, he would pay for them to fly out to Jersey for a long weekend, all expenses paid. Dave had often gone out there with his football club for pre-season training when he was a professional player and he had fond memories of those years.

As a kid he'd kick a ball around the streets near his home and dream of one day playing for Man United, Leeds or Newcastle. He was a football-mad kid who dreamt of football stardom; he would get up in the morning, grab a ball and have a kick-about while eating a piece of toast. On the way to school he'd dribble a tennis ball or golf ball along the pavement, and once there he and his mates would pick sides and have a match, only ending when the bell rang and everyone filed into school. At 3.30 p.m. he'd rush home and kick a ball up against the wall in the garden, or his mates would come round and they'd go off to the park and play until it got dark. When he wasn't kicking a football he was reading about it, he must have bought every magazine that came out, and had cut out and pasted pictures of his favourite players on his bedroom wall.

When he was twelve Dave was spotted by a scout from a south-coast team. He went along to some trials and eventually signed up on schoolboy terms for them. After a few years he was taken on as an apprentice, and then he was told by the assistant manager that the club were going to offer him a contract as a professional. He was over the moon; he was only seventeen years old, and he was about to make a living from the game he loved. But his joy wasn't to last long. The board of directors sacked the manager and his backroom staff, a new manager was brought in, and as the saying goes, a new broom sweeps clean. The new manager, under pressure from the chairman to get results, had a massive clearout and Dave was one of those shown the door.

He was devastated; his world seemed to have fallen apart overnight. He went back home to his parents' house, unable to face his friends and the outside world. After moping about for a few weeks, he and a good mate decided to go off backpacking around Europe. Dave got bored after a few months of grape-picking in southern France and decided to move on to Spain, where he worked in a bar. His mate returned home after a while but Dave stayed on and ended up running the place. In his time there he celebrated both his eighteenth and twenty-first birthdays, only returning to England one Christmas. While he was at home his dad was taken ill and rushed into hospital with a suspected heart attack. Dave and his mum sat at his bedside for days and nights on end. One night Dave told his mum to go home and get some rest, have a good sleep in her own bed. Reluctantly, she agreed, and Dave stayed to hold his father's hand. He must have dozed off, but something made him jump out of his sleep. His dad had suddenly released his grip on Dave's hand and his face had gone ashen-white. The emptiness and pain that came with the realisation his father had passed away was indescribable.

Dave stayed with his mum for a few weeks after the funeral and then returned to his job in Spain. A couple of weeks after his return his mum paid him a surprise visit. They went out to dinner one evening and after the meal she handed Dave an envelope. Inside was a cheque for ten thousand pounds. 'What's this?' he asked her, shocked and bemused.

'It's for you, your dad left it in his will.'

'What about you?'

'Your dad was always thinking of what would happen when he went, and he made sure I'd be all right.'

'Mum. What can I say, but thank you?'

'Don't thank me, thank your father.'

He looked up to the heavens, clasped his hands in prayer and kissed his mum. 'Thank you Dad, thank you.'

Dave invested the money in a bar further along the coast, down on the Costa del Sol, where he stayed for another six years before selling up, making a good profit, and returning home.

The players were meeting up for a light breakfast and a team talk at 11 a.m. At midday Dave was going to put them through a light training session, then it would be on to the luxury coach he'd hired for the day to transport the players to the Gas Board sports ground, where the game was being played. Half the estate was expected to turn out to watch the game, so they would have plenty of noisy support.

The semi-final of the cup had been a memorable two-legged

affair against a team who were known troublemakers on and off the field. They, like the Tavern, were a pub team. The first leg had finished with the Tavern losing a close game, 1–0. Both teams had had a player sent off and the referee had booked four players from each side. At the end of the game, players and supporters from both sides had swapped insults and punches and the police had to be called to restore order. The manager of the opposition was arrested for threatening behaviour and some of the Tavern's players' cars were stoned as they pulled away from the changing-rooms.

A fortnight later in the second leg, played at home, nearly the whole estate had turned up to support their side. The Tavern scored in the second minute, sending the home crowd wild with delight. A few fans ran onto the pitch to congratulate the players, and some saw this as an opportunity to have a dig at the opposition. A couple of the players were kicked and punched before the ref, with the help of Dave, the manager, cleared the pitch and play was restarted. The score remained the same right up until the 89th minute, when the ref controversially gave a penalty to the visitors. A corner had been floated in from the left into a crowded penalty area. One of the Tavern's defenders headed the ball out, and then fell to the ground. The ball was played straight back in, and as he was getting to his feet, it struck his hand. The visitors appealed in sheer desperation for a penalty. To almost everyone's surprise, the ref blew his whistle and pointed to the spot.

The crowd were incensed and more unpleasantness and threats were exchanged. Order was restored as the ref blew his whistle. The penalty-taker confidently strode up and hit the ball low and hard, aiming for the corner of the net. The Tavern's keeper threw himself full-length across the goal and palmed the ball onto the outside of the post and out of play for a corner.

The penalty-taker put his head in his hands and dropped to his knees. The keeper was jumped on and sent sprawling before being buried under a pile of bodies as his team-mates ruffled his hair and kissed and cuddled him. Before there was time to take the corner, the ref put his whistle to his mouth and blew for full-time. The crowd swarmed on, and a few of their players were tripped or knocked down. The rest of the opposition legged it off the pitch for the safety of the changing-rooms while the home team were carried shoulder-high around the pitch, before being stripped of their shirts and shorts by over-zealous souvenir hunters. You would have thought it was Wembley and 1966 all over again! The celebrations went on long into the night, with players and fans dancing on the bar in the Tavern.

A few days after the game Dave received a letter from the chairman of the league committee, who wrote informing him that the opposition had sent in a formal complaint about the Tavern's players and their fans' behaviour. Dave was called up to a meeting with the chairman and told that if there were any more incidents like this, the team would be thrown out of the league and expelled from all cup competitions. That was why it was so important that the players and fans alike behaved themselves at today's game.

The team bus pulled up outside the ground and the players stepped off and walked into the warm sunshine. The opposition were already having a kick-about on the pitch. The Gas Board, obviously with money to spare, had built a decent ground, with covered seating on both sides of the ground, which quickly began to fill with fans from both sides. Dave took the players into the changing-rooms and ran through what was expected of them one last time, emphasising that there was to be no repeat of the aggro that had marred the semi-final games. He told the players that the game was being watched by some high-ranking officials from the league and said he'd heard word that a couple of First Division teams were sending down scouts to have a look at a couple of players. The team looked at one another and laughed. Earl joked, 'Today the Gas Board ground, next season Old Trafford, Highbury or even Stamford Bridge. I may go out to Italy and sign up for an Italian side, perhaps Inter Milan or Juventus.'

'Fray Bentos more like,' said Dave, throwing his number nine shirt at him from the kit bag in the middle of the room.

The referee came in and introduced himself. He asked to speak to the new captain, Keith, and explained to Keith that he wouldn't put up with any dissent and that he expected a good clean game. He wished everyone the best of luck and said he would see them out on the field of play in ten minutes. Dave was taking this game very seriously and began to gee his players up as they queued to leave the dressing-room. Some players jumped up and down on the spot, while others kicked footballs against the wall. Dave reminded them all that in a few weeks' time they could all be lying around a swimming pool in sunny Jersey. 'Come on lads, let's get out there and get into them.' 'Yeah!' shouted the players in reply as they ran out, full of confidence.

The two teams took to the field to a rousing reception from both stands, which were packed to near capacity. The referee and his two linesmen, dressed in black, strode out into the centre circle. He shook hands with both captains and spun the coin to see who would kick off or have the choice of which way to kick. The Tavern won the toss and chose to kick with the sun on their backs. The referee checked the linesmen were ready, put the whistle to his lips and blew for the game to get underway. From the kick-off Earl played a ball out on to the right wing, where the Tavern's full-back Danny had found some space. He moved the ball down the line and floated in a beautiful curling cross. The keeper jumped for it, under pressure from Earl, but was dazzled by the sunshine, causing him to flap at the ball. He looked like he'd got it covered – for a split second he had the ball in his grasp – but next thing he was fumbling at thin air. Earl pounced on the loose ball and toe-poked it into the empty net.

He raced around the back of the goal and celebrated with the crowds standing there. The rest of the team dived on him and he was buried at the bottom of a pile of jubilant bodies. 'Get off for fuck's sake, I can't breathe,' he cried, gasping for air. Everyone was kissing him and rubbing his huge afro. He managed to get himself free and stood up, hands aloft, as he walked back to the centre circle. He could see his mum and dad hugging one another in the stands. He gave his dad the thumbs up and his father waved back. Earl studied the sea of faces, wondering if he could pick out any of the scouts from the league clubs. Dave leapt from the dugout and barked instructions to his team: 'Keep it tight lads, the game's not won yet, there's another 89 minutes to play.'

Earl had another couple of half chances just before half-time but failed to put any of them away. The referee blew for half-time and the players trooped off for their well-earned slice of orange or a hot, sweet cup of tea. A couple of them took the opportunity to have a quick fag. Dave was well pleased with their first-half performance. 'You played some wonderful football and knocked the ball around well. Keep it nice and tight in the second half and don't give nothing silly away, and I can see us winning this game.' A couple of players had minor knocks and strains and Dave and another lad got to work with the Deep Heat. Nobby Clark, the team's giant 6 ft 8 in. goalkeeper and a local hero after that semi-final penalty save, joked that if someone had their leg hanging on by a thread Dave would simply rub some liniment into it and tell them to get out there, stop moaning and run it off. They'd feel much better after a couple of minutes! He swore by the stuff.

The second half got underway and the opposition took the game by the scruff of the neck. They mounted wave after wave of attacks and were unlucky not to be on level terms. They hit the foot of a post from a direct free kick and had a couple of shots cleared off the line. Now they were doing all the pressing and the Tavern knew they were riding their luck, it really should have been 1–1 by that time. 'Come on lads, for fuck's sake,' shouted Dave from the touch-line. He looked at his watch for the thousandth time. There was still nearly twenty minutes left to play.

The Tavern hadn't had a shot on target in this half when Earl, who'd been relatively quiet, picked up the ball just on the halfway line and went on a mazy run. He beat two, then three, then four players, and looked up to release the ball to someone. There was no one there. He was on the edge of the opposition's penalty area and decided to have a crack. But as he pulled his right leg back to shoot, CRASH! He was sent sprawling to the ground by a tackle from behind. He picked himself up and spat out dirt and mud, putting his fingers to his mouth to check that he hadn't lost any front teeth. The player who had tackled him was called over and spoken to by the referee. He walked away grinning. 'Next time, black boy, I'll break your fucking neck.' Earl walked over to him and stuck his face forward so that his nose was touching the other bloke's and they went eyeball to eyeball. 'Try it you white rarse clarte, you lickle monkey rarse clart, I'll kick you up ya mudder's clarte.'

'Get fucked jungle bunny,' said the bloke, taking a step back. 'Why don't you fuck off back to your own country?'

Earl clenched his fist as his team-mates stepped in between them. 'What do you mean, fuck off back to my own country? Where am I going to fuck off to? This is my country.'

Players from both sides laughed.

'Why can't you speak English then?' asked the bloke who'd just fouled him.

'I do,' said Earl.

'No you don't,' said the bloke. 'You just jumped up and started speaking some foreign language, like African or something.'

Earl laughed. When he lost his temper he did copy his father and shout and curse in Jamaican slang.

'Cool it,' said the ref, 'or you'll both go in the book.'

Earl was awarded a free kick for the foul. He grabbed the ball and placed it down on the muddy grass. The opposition set up a five-man wall as their keeper shouted furiously behind them to move more to the right. Earl took a dozen paces backwards and tapped his left boot on the ground to shake off any excess mud. The ref indicated that the free kick was in fact direct and blew his whistle.

The wall stood tall and firm with their hands cupped in front of their nuts for protection. Earl let go a thundering shot which first rose up and then dipped down to the right of the wall, curling into the corner of the net. The players and fans went wild. Earl did a somersault with delight. Even the referee ran alongside him on the way back to the halfway line and congratulated him on a great strike.

In the last ten minutes the Tavern players stroked the ball cockily around as all the heart and fight went out of the opposition. During injury time, Earl added a third goal and got his hat-trick. At the final whistle the fans rushed onto the pitch to hail their heroes. Wendy ran down from the stand, hugged

Dave and told him how proud she was of him. She had tears rolling down her cheeks. 'I'm so happy for you,' she said as the players and supporters kissed her and shook Dave's hand.

Dave was as proud as punch and even he had a tear in his eye. He couldn't believe that less than three years ago this team didn't even exist. This was Dave's dream – to one day run a team that would win the county cup and challenge for the league, and he had done it. Steve, the ex-captain, sat there expressionless. He and Dave had had a row about his lack of effort in one game and they had nearly come to blows, after Dave had called him a big-headed lazy bastard. They squared up to one another and one of the players held Dave's arms so that he wouldn't hit Steve. Steve saw this as a golden opportunity to give Dave a dig and walloped him twice in the face. 'Come on cunt!' shouted Steve, confident that he had the upper hand and could finish the job. Larry, who was holding Dave back, released his grip and the two of them went toe-to-toe. Dave unloaded some heavy shots to Steve's head and sent him reeling backwards into the dressing-room door, pummelling him with some merciless body shots, and caught him with a peach of an uppercut to his jaw. Steve fell to the floor, blood trickling from the corner of his mouth. 'I've had enough,' he whispered, unable to talk with a mouth full of blood and broken teeth. From that day on Steve had no longer been welcome anywhere near the football team or the pub, but today he had obviously come along to gloat if the team had lost.

Back in the dressing-room the boys were diving into the water-filled bath, still in their kits. The champagne corks were popping and Dave was thrown into the water fully clothed. A steady stream of people came into the dressing-room to offer their congratulations. Somehow Kerry, fully clothed for a change, was thrown into the bath and emerged minus her top and bra.

The celebrations continued on the journey back to the pub. As the victorious players stepped off the coach, a huge crowd gathered and cheered. They applauded the players as they entered under a huge 'well done lads' banner hanging from the front of the pub. The Dave Clark Five's 'Glad All Over' boomed from the speakers. It was a real carnival atmosphere, with everyone for once mixing together. The DJ turned the music down and Dave got up on stage to thank everyone for their fantastic support. Wendy stood by his side and held his hand tightly. As Earl stood chatting with his parents and going through his goals, analysing each one again and again, a man walked up to him and introduced himself as a scout working for Fulham Football Club. He asked Earl if he would like to come along and have a trial for the club. Earl's dad replied that he and the family would sit down and talk about it. The scout said he understood the situation and that there was no rush to make a decision, and left them a business card. The party continued until the early hours of the morning and the following day there were plenty of people walking around nursing some seriously sore heads.

The Tavern clinched the league title the following weekend with a convincing 5–0 win. The following weekend the team went off for their long weekend in Jersey. Dave and Wendy both went along, with Wendy even calling it their second honeymoon. One night back at the hotel after going out on the town, a few of the lads got a bit rowdy and the night porter had to knock on the door of one of their rooms and ask them to consider the other guests and keep the noise down. No one took any notice, so the police were called and when they arrived a few of the lads were madly running around the hotel corridors with no clothes on, banging on the other guests' doors. The hotel switchboard was on meltdown. One elderly couple complained that someone had banged on their door shouting for them to get out because there was a fire, and when they had opened it a naked man had sprayed them from head to foot with white foam from a fire extinguisher and then run off. Someone else had gone into the kitchen and left a nasty surprise in a frying pan, with a note beside it that read 'please warm up in the morning'. Ten of the party were arrested and thrown off the island. The only other downside of the trip was that Dave and Wendy had had to leave Kerry in charge of the pub. Still, the sale of condoms from the machine in the men's toilets was sure to rise.

Back at the pub the following week, Wendy returned from a shopping trip with the girls one afternoon and asked if Dave could leave what he was doing behind the bar and come upstairs for five minutes. A huge grin spread across his face and he rubbed his hands together – he knew what that meant. It didn't happen very often, but sometimes when Wendy had been out shopping with the girls she would drag him off upstairs when she got back. His joy was short-lived; she told him on the way up to forget any ideas he might have of an afternoon of hot passion.

Wendy threw her bags of shopping onto the settee and plonked down beside them. She kicked her shoes off and pulled her feet up onto the cushion. 'Dave,' she said, looking right at him, 'I'll come straight to the point. I need a break.'

The blood drained from Dave's face and tears welled up in his eyes. 'But, but,' he stuttered, 'I thought we were getting on well. Is it something I've said or done to Kerry?'

'Dave,' she said, nearly laughing, 'I'm not talking about us splitting up or me moving out, I'm talking about me and the girls going away on holiday for a week. You know, somewhere hot like Spain or Portugal, a week in the sun will do me the world of good.'

'But why?' asked Dave, relieved that his wife wasn't about to desert him but still unsure why she needed to get away from him. 'I know, why don't you let me go to the travel agents first thing in the morning and I'll book us a nice romantic long weekend in Paris.' He smiled and looked at her for approval. Dave sat down next to her and held her hand. 'What's brought all this on?'

'It's been hard work getting this place up and running and I feel that I need a break. It doesn't mean I've gone off you or don't love you anymore, it's just that I need to have a change of scenery and recharge my batteries. When I was having a chat over a cup of coffee with some of the girls, one of them suggested that we all go off somewhere for a week's break. I just thought "why not, I've got the money so why not go for it". We haven't done anything about booking anything yet, it was only suggested about an hour ago.'

'So who's going?'

'Me, Lynn and Sharon.'

'You're fucking joking, you expect me to let you go on holiday without me, with two of the biggest slappers God created? No, I ain't having it. If you think I'd be happy about you going away with them two then you must think I'm stark raving fucking mad.'

'Don't you trust me?'

'Yeah, of course I trust you, but I wouldn't trust the other two.'

'Well, there's your answer.'

'What do you mean?'

'You're married to me, not the other two.'

Dave shook his head. 'Of all the people in this world, why would you want to go on holiday with those two?'

'Because they're a laugh, and they're good company.'

'What will people on the estate say when they find out

you've gone on holiday with them? I'll be a laughing stock, I'll never hear the last of it.'

'Dave, all you're doing is listening to idle gossip, rumours and chit-chat, they're not that bad.'

'You're having a laugh! Not that bad my arse! One's got three kids by three different men and it's rumoured that half the men on the estate have hung out the back of her, and the other one's husband's inside, she runs a free weekend guesthouse for any men under the age of 45 who'll shag her, and you want me to give you the green light to go away with them? Well, the answer's no!' And with that he got up and stormed out of the room, slamming the door behind him.

Downstairs Dave began serving the customers as usual.

'Pint of lager please Dave.'

'You're in early tonight, Alf.'

'Yeah, I gotta open up the centre for tonight's bingo.'

Wendy appeared behind the bar carrying a suitcase.

'Off somewhere nice?' asked Alf.

'Only to my sister's down in Hampshire.'

Dave shouted for Tom the barman to look after things, took the case from Wendy and guided her back upstairs. 'Right,' he said, 'just to prove how much I trust and love you, I'm going to let you go on this holiday, but if I find out that you've been cheating on me then I'll be the one walking out of here.' She threw her arms around him and kissed him. 'I mean it, if you shit on me I'm out of here.'

'Dave, I just need a break with some female company, that's all. I promise I'll be good.'

'I must get back downstairs and see how Tom's coping.'

'He can manage, come on, let's have a cuddle in bed for five minutes.' She pushed Dave into the bedroom, undid the zipper on his jeans and dropped to her knees.

'Right, there's your tickets for the aircraft and your insurance details, these give you all the information you need. If you have a medical problem and have to see a doctor or attend a hospital while you're abroad, please keep them with you at all times. Be at the airport two hours before the departure time. Any questions?' The travel agent handed over the envelope containing the relevant documents and wished them a happy holiday, 'I wish I was coming with you, I bet you'll have a great time.'

'We'll squeeze you in if you want,' said Sharon.

'You can hide in my suitcase, no one would notice,' said Lynn.

The three girls came out of the travel agents and into a downpour of torrential rain. Wendy pulled an umbrella from her shopping bag and the three of them sheltered beneath it. 'Just think, this time next week we'll be lying on a beach in Torremolinos and leave all this poxy weather behind.'

'Sunny Spain, here we come,' said Sharon.

'Spanish men watch out,' said Lynn.

'Last one to the Wimpy buys the coffees.' Wendy quickly folded the umbrella down and sprinted across the road in the rain. The other two never had a chance.

The week before they went Dave couldn't do enough for her and followed Wendy around like a little puppy dog. Every night he made love to her like he'd never done before; usually he'd have one shot, come, then roll off and fall asleep snoring like a pig. This past week he'd been doing things they'd never tried before, plus he was banging away like a champion and lasting more than two minutes. Wendy loved it. 'Perhaps I'll book another holiday!' she joked.

A day before the girls were due to go they had a bit of a scare, and it seemed that their plans were about to fall apart. It turned out that Lynn didn't have a passport or the money to pay for one. Sharon, who was financing the trip for them both, had to go up to the passport office in central London with her and queue for ten hours, along with Lynn's kids, who had to take a day off school because there would be no one to pick them up later. Lynn's mum had refused to have them, saying she would be looking after them for the whole of the next week and today she was putting her feet up and having a rest. A lull before the storm, was how she described it. She was obviously angry that Lynn had gone and booked a holiday without speaking to her about it first.

With Lynn now the proud owner of a British passport, the thought of getting on a plane and flying off abroad began to make her nervous. She sat opposite her children on the tube journey back to south London and for the first time realised just how much they meant to her and how much she'd miss them in the next week. Since they'd been born, besides the odd night here and there, they'd never been apart. It would be strange not to have their smiling faces beaming at her every morning. On the other hand, she'd never had any quality time on her own to relax and have a glass of wine or read a book. Thinking back, the last holiday she'd had was nearly twenty years ago, and that was in a caravan just outside Eastbourne with her mum, dad and nan. It had rained nearly the whole week.

When she got back home Lynn bathed the kids and got them ready for bed. Then she started packing the suitcase her mum had lent her. Nan was staying over that night so there'd be someone to get the kids fed and ready for school. She had an early start in the morning, Sharon was picking her up at seven and then they were meeting Wendy at the pub. They had nearly an hour's drive down to Gatwick airport. She'd managed to save fifty pounds to take with her and she promised the kids she'd bring them back something nice, kissed them all goodnight and told them how much she loved them. As she turned their bedroom light off and told them she'd see them all next week, she wondered if she was doing the right thing.

Lynn wiped a tear from her eye, put the kettle on and made herself and her mum a cup of tea, then carried it in from the kitchen and put it on the coffee table.

'All right?'

'Yeah.'

'Looking forward to your holiday?'

'Yeah.'

'Nervous?'

'Yeah.'

'You'll be fine,' said Lynn's mum, setting her cup down and putting her arm around her daughter. Before she could say 'you go and enjoy yourself', Lynn burst into tears. 'Mum, what if something dreadful happens, like the plane crashes or I get knocked down by a car?'

'Don't be so silly, millions of people fly off on holiday now, they say it's safer travelling by air then it is by road.' Nan handed Lynn a tissue to wipe her tears and dry her eyes. 'You'll be fine, the kids are with me. Go on, go off and have some fun, you're only young once.'

'Thanks Mum.'

Lynn was up, bathed and dressed and had her make-up on when Sharon turned up just before seven.

'What the fuck have you got in this case?' said Sharon as she struggled with it to the lift.

'The cab's waiting downstairs, you'd have thought he would have come up and given us a hand, the miserable bastard.'

Lynn also had a holdall, a vanity case and a handbag. 'How long you going for?'

'Well, I want to look my best.'

'Have you got your passport?' asked Sharon as the lift door slid shut.

'Yes, it's in me handbag.'

'Are you sure?'

'Yes, I've checked and double-checked that I've got everything.'

'Good, right, let's go then driver,' said Sharon to the cabbie as she climbed into the front seat and slammed the door. They pulled slowly away. Suddenly a woman in a dressing-gown came from nowhere and threw herself on the bonnet.

'Jesus fucking Christ!' said the driver. 'Who the fuck is that?'

'Mum, what's up?' said Lynn jumping out of the car. Her mum struggled for breath and had to wait a few seconds before she spoke. She pulled something from her dressing-gown pocket. 'You forgot this!' She handed Lynn her passport. 'I don't think you would have got very far without it.'

'Sorry Mum,' said Lynn.

'Scatty cow,' muttered the driver.

'Oi, you watch ya mouth!' said Sharon. 'That's my mate.'

The driver went bright and mumbled that he was sorry. They picked up Wendy and her two suitcases from the pub and the driver loaded up her cases and handbags as she squeezed into the back with the other two. 'What's up with the seat in the front?' asked the driver.

'You're too bleedin' grumpy, so we'd rather all sit in the back.'

'Dave only wanted to come to the airport with us,' Wendy told the other two.

'Silly sod.'

'I've given him the flight number and he reckons he's going to meet us.'

'What, don't he trust ya?'

'Of course he doesn't, I'm going on holiday with you two!'

They arrived at Gatwick and unloaded their cases themselves as the driver sat behind the steering wheel. 'It's all right, we can manage,' said Sharon sarcastically.

'You just sit there you fat lazy bastard,' snarled Wendy. The man stared back at her. 'It'll be the last time we use your company, you're fucking useless, no wonder people are using black cabs these days. They may be a little bit dearer, but at least the drivers are helpful and polite, not like you, you fucking pig.' She chucked a pound note through the window and it landed on his lap. He picked up his two-way radio and held it to his mouth. 'Lima two, nine to base, have dropped off three more than happy punters, returning to office, over.'

'Get fucked, you tramp!' shouted Sharon as the car pulled off with a cloud of black smoke rising from the exhaust. A two-fingered salute came from the dropped window of the car. 'Up yours Lard Arse!' she yelled back at the top of her voice.

The girls were in fits of giggles when they realised they were not alone – hundreds of people were milling around the concourse, and many were standing there open-mouthed, not believing what they'd just witnessed. 'What you looking at, you nosey old cows?' Sharon snapped at two old pensioners.

They found the airline they were flying with and checked their bags in. 'He's a poof,' said Sharon, talking loudly about the man who was weighing their bags and tying flight labels to the handles. Next it was through passport control. 'Good morning ladies, may I see your passports and flight tickets.' He looked at Wendy's. 'Off somewhere nice?' Before she could answer he handed back her passport. 'Thank you ma'am, next please. Good morning.' He looked at the photo on Sharon's passport and handed it back to her. 'Hello,' he said to Lynn, staring into her big blue eyes, 'off somewhere nice?'

'Spain,' said Lynn, 'and I'm very nervous, it's the first time I've flown.'

'You've nothing to worry about, it's the safest form of travel. I was in the Royal Air Force for twenty years before I retired due to injury.'

'What happened?' Lynn asked, imagining the man standing tall and handsome in his uniform, a handlebar moustache covering most of his lower face.

'I was shot down over France in the last few days of the war.'

'Well, it just shows it ain't as safe as you and some other people say.'

He laughed at her naïvety. 'Have a good holiday.'

Off they went to the bar. Wendy ordered three large gin and Slimline tonics as the three dropped their handbags to their feet and pulled themselves up onto bar stools. Sharon lifted her glass and took a long gulp. 'Fucking hell, I needed that.' She finished the rest of it off with the next swallow. 'Same again please mate,' she said to the barman. He poured the drinks out and she handed the money over. 'Get that down ya Lynn, that'll settle your nerves, you've hardly said a word since we picked you up. What's up, you frightened or something?'

Lynn smiled nervously.

'We'll have to watch the screen to see what gate we depart from,' Wendy fretted.

'There's plenty of time, Wend, don't panic,' said Sharon, lighting up a cigarette as she polished off her drink. 'Whose round is it next?'

Lynn bent down, took her purse from her bag and sorted out enough change to pay for it. 'Same again is it?'

The other two nodded.

'Here, please allow me to get these,' said a deep voice at her side. Lynn looked to her right. Standing there was a well-dressed man in a suit and tie. 'Thank you,' said Lynn, unsure of what to say next. 'I'm Ian,' said the man, holding out his hand for Lynn to shake, but before she could answer him, Sharon stepped in. 'Hello Ian, I'm Sharon, pleased to meet you.' She leant forward and kissed him on the cheek. 'Did you say you'd like to buy us girls a drink?'

'Yes, yes, by all means. What would you like?'

Wendy and Lynn still had full glasses. 'Three triple gins with ice and Slimline tonic, please, Ian,' said Sharon unashamedly.

'Right, three triple gins coming up.' He ordered the drinks, plus one for himself. The barman poured them and he handed the money over. 'Cheers everyone,' he said, raising his glass. Sharon downed hers in one. 'Steady on Sharon,' said Wendy. 'We'll have to carry you onto the plane at this rate.'

'Fuck it, we're on holiday ain't we?'

'We ain't got there yet!'

'And we won't if she carries on like that,' said Lynn, not quite believing just how much booze Sharon was consuming.

'Our flight's come up!' said Wendy, who'd been keeping one eye on the board all the time. 'We're boarding at gate number 13.'

'Fucking hell, that's lucky,' said Sharon, slurring her words and talking loudly, to the annoyance of the other passengers around her. 'There's no rush, we've time for another quick one. What's the hurry?'

'I don't want one,' said the other two girls as the bar began to empty and passengers made their way down to the departure gates. Wendy and Lynn climbed down off their stools and picked their bags up. 'Come on Sharon, we've got to go.' They began to walk off. 'Thanks for the drink Ian, it was nice meeting you,' they both said.

'My pleasure,' he said. 'Now, can I get you another drink, Sharon?'

'Yes please, the same again. I'll catch up with you,' she shouted to the other two as they disappeared down a long corridor.

Wendy stopped, turned around and motioned to Sharon to hurry up. 'I'll be two minutes,' she shouted back. She finished her drink. 'Fancy a quick one?' said Ian as Sharon noticed him taking a sneaky look down her top. 'Yeah, let's have a drink first and then you can do what you like.'

'Will Mrs Sharon Smith please come to gate number 13, where the flight to Malaga airport is about to depart. Last call for Mrs Sharon Smith.'

'Fucking hell, where is she?' said Wendy.

'Probably lying in a drunken stupor somewhere,' said Lynn, worried about her. 'Shall we go and look for her?'

'What, and miss the flight? No, let's get on board. It would take us ten minutes to walk all the way back up to the bar we were in.' They handed their boarding passes over to the flight dispatcher who made arrangements for the baggage handlers to find and offload Sharon's bags. Before they could open the hold, Sharon came along the departure jetty in a wheel chair. She winked at Wendy and Lynn as a care assistant helped her from the wheel chair and in through the doors of the plane, and helped her into her seat. 'I've just told this lovely young man all about my heart condition, and how I needed a small sherry to calm my nerves. He so kindly pushed me all the way from the departure lounge.'

The aircraft's doors closed and the plane taxied out onto the runway. The engines revved up and it thundered along. Lynn looked at Wendy, who squeezed her hand as the plane began to lift up. Soon they were up in the clouds, and the crew left their seats and began serving drinks. 'See, there's nothing to

162

it,' said Wendy. Lynn smiled and began to relax, and turned to Sharon, who by this time was fast asleep.

After a smooth flight, they were touching down in southern Spain within a couple of hours. Wendy shook Sharon, who had slept her way through the flight. 'What, what?' she said, coming around from her booze-fuelled siesta, stretching her arms above her head and letting out a loud yawn. 'Jesus, I'm starving,' she said. 'Is dinner being served?'

The other two laughed. 'Look out the window,' said Lynn.

'Shit, we're on the ground, haven't we left yet?'

'You've been asleep for over two hours,' Wendy told her.

'Fucking hell,' said Sharon, rubbing her forehead. 'My head is thumping, did we drink a lot at Gatwick?'

'Drink a lot? Don't you remember, we left you with Ian and you nearly missed the flight!'

'Who the fuck is Ian?'

'The nice young man we met in the departure lounge bar.'

'Fuck me, I must have been pissed because I don't remember him.'

'Well, you were knocking the large gins back a bit lively.'

They disembarked from the aircraft, and the heat hit them immediately. 'Ain't it fucking hot!'

'I don't think I can handle this for a week.'

'Good job we never booked for two.'

'Will you two stop moaning, we've only just got here,' said Wendy.

They made their way to the customs desk where they showed the man in the glass box their passports. He looked at Sharon's photo and laughed before handing it back to her, then looked at Wendy in her low-cut top, opened her passport and laughed again. He opened the door of the booth he was in and shouted out to his colleagues who were sitting in a side room,

THE ESTATE

'Rapido viene aqui y mira estos tres puercos.' A couple of heads looked around the door and also started laughing.'El infierno de fucking ellos son feos!' More laughter.

The girls smiled and went off to reclaim their baggage 'What was all that about?' asked Lynn as she struggled to get her cases off the moving conveyor belt.

'I ain't got a clue,' said Sharon, 'but they seem to be having a laugh.'

'At your expense,' said a lady standing next to them, who had heard and understood every word the customs man had said. 'They were calling you three girls pigs and he was saying to his mates how ugly he thought you were.'

'Cheeky bastard,' said Sharon, 'he was greasy and had a pock-marked face, the fucking ugly dago bastard. I've a good mind to go back there and tell him what I think of him, the fucking tosser, how dare he say that about us. I'll have him thrown out of the country.'

'I think you'll find he lives here,' said Lynn, trying not to laugh at Sharon's outburst.

They were met outside the airport by a holiday rep and pointed in the direction of a coach which they were told to board after an hour's wait in the burning sun. 'Good morning Ladies and Gentlemen,' said a voice from a microphone down at the front of the coach. 'I hope you had a pleasant flight and I'd like to take this opportunity of welcoming you all to sunny Spain. The weather over the last few days has been in the mid-eighties, so I hope you've all packed your sun cream. My name is Miguel and I'm the rep at the hotel you'll be staying at; everyone on this coach should be, according to my paperwork, staying at the Mediterranean Sol hotel. If you're not then you've a long walk back to the airport!' A few of the old grunters at the front laughed at Miguel's attempt at humour. The girls laughed, but at him because they thought he was a bit of a prat. He waffled on and on about drinking water and mosquito bites, and exchange rates and tours. 'Fuck me, how do you shut him up?' said Sharon, still half-pissed and starting to get a hangover.

'Do you mind being quiet,' said an old man sitting with his wife just in front of the girls, 'Miguel is quite interesting if you would only bother to listen.'

'Bollocks, he's a fucking bore,' said Sharon as Lynn and Wendy hid their faces in their hands.

The coach pulled up outside the hotel and it was nice to get off, stretch their legs and get some fresh air. 'Please pick up your cases and follow me,' said the courier, marching off without checking if anyone was following behind her. A trail of people snaked slowly behind her, struggling with their cases. They followed for a couple of hundred yards along an unfinished path which led through what looked like a building site, and squeezed past a huge pile of sand and bags of cement and plaster. 'Mind your heads on the scaffolding as you go through into reception,' said the courier as she stood at the main entrance guiding people in. The girls looked at one another, gobsmacked at the state of the place. At the reception desk they were rudely received by a moaning Spaniard, who refused to talk English. He handed the girls the key to their room and pointed at the stairs. 'Let's take the lift,' said Wendy. 'These bags are far too heavy to drag up those stairs.'

'The lift is not in operation as yet,' said Miguel, seeming proud of the fact that the hotel had a lift even though it wasn't working. 'Leave your bags here and I'll have a man bring them to your room.'

The girls, sweating bucketloads, dragged themselves up to the sixth floor, where their room was. They opened the door and pulled back the curtains of the darkened room. When they walked out onto the balcony, a man less than six feet away smiled at them as he sat at the controls of a huge tower crane. 'I don't believe it,' said Lynn. 'We're living in the middle of a bloody building site.' Just as she said that, a siren sounded and machinery started up, cement mixers came to life and pneumatic drills hissed and pissed out ear-shattering noise. The girls shut the blinds and drew the curtains. That seemed to cut out a bit of the racket, so they lay down on their beds. They'd had a hard day and it wasn't long before all of them were fast asleep.

Sharon woke up first and decided to take a shower while the others were still asleep. She got undressed and turned the water on. It poured out with great force, but the only problem was it was stone cold. Sharon tried adjusting the temperature, but it was no good, it wasn't getting any warmer. She leant out of the shower and grabbed her shampoo from the small bag she'd carried up with her, poured some out and rubbed it into her hair – and then the shower stopped. 'Fucking arse-holes!' She banged the rusty metal pipe with her fist. Nothing, not even a drip.

Wrapping a towel round her, she went marching down the stairs to the reception. Sitting at the bar were Miguel and the grumpy hotel manager. They both saw her coming and sniggered. 'What the fuck are you laughing at, you pair of fucking wankers?' Miguel went red. 'What sort of country is this, when you're taking a shower and the fucking water cuts out?'

'Please, I am so sorry,' Miguel apologised, 'I will send a man up straight away.'

'That wouldn't be the one you said would be bringing our cases up over two hours ago, would it? Because if it is, could someone stick a rocket up his arse to liven him up?'

Both men laughed as she called both of them wankers again and stormed back upstairs. Miguel shouted after her that she was in Spain now and the pace of life was somewhat slower than that of England. When she got back upstairs the other two were awake. She was telling them the story when the first of the suitcases turned up. 'What, you bringing up one a day?' she sarcastically asked. The man disappeared and came back with another about half an hour later. 'Why don't you strap them to a snail's back, it'll be quicker,' she joked.

'I no speak English,' said the man, making a quick getaway.

In the end, they somehow managed to get washed and dressed for dinner, and what a palaver that was. They waited for ages for the food and when it did turn up it was stone cold, Lynn's salad had ants crawling in and out of it, and even the ice-cream dessert had melted before it got to them. The following morning there was a fight for the toilet as all three had dodgy bellies. They decided to give the hotel food a miss and eat out instead for the rest of the week.

Wherever they went, the girls were besieged by men of all ages, shapes and sizes. Some wanted to run away with them, others claimed undying love and proposed marriage, while others were a bit more honest and upfront, and said they'd love to shag them. Sharon did her best to oblige and never slept in the same bed twice. Lynn was a good girl and although she danced with a few blokes, and kissed and cuddled a couple of them, while she was away she was very good. She thought of her three kids back home with Mum and the trouble drunken sex could bring. She'd even bought a paperback at the airport, so she would often curl up for the night with just her book for company and engross herself in the happy, romantic story, something she hadn't done since she was a kid and had illicitly read books under the bedcovers by torchlight.

Wendy had also stayed true to her word. Again, although she

had slow-danced with a couple of blokes and had a bit of a kiss and a cuddle, she wouldn't allow it to go any further. She did meet a man her age in a club one night, and quite fancied him. He was both charming and handsome, but the evening she was supposed to meet him she was laid up with a touch of sunstroke and Benidorm belly. She spent that night in between the toilet and the bathroom sink, and the whole of the next day she felt unsteady, sick, shaky and ill, so that scuppered her plans of getting well serviced! Still, at least she didn't have to lie to Dave when she got home, because her behaviour hadn't been that bad.

As the week drew to a close and they packed their cases to go home, they agreed they'd all in their own ways had a nice holiday. Back at the airport, checking their bags in, they said goodbye to Miguel, the housewife's favourite. As it had turned out he wasn't such a bad bloke, all the old girls loved him and they all told him they'd be back to see him next year.

They showed their passports and the man flicked through them. Two others stood behind him chatting, but stopped as the girls approached. 'Hizolo goza su tiempo en Espana?' said the man, handing the girls their passports back.

'Sorry, what was that?' said Sharon.

One of the men stepped forward from behind. 'My colleague doesn't speak English and he was just asking you ladies if you had enjoyed your time here in Spain?'

Sharon smiled. 'Please thank your friend for being so kind and tell him from me and my friends that I have had a marvellous time, an absolutely wonderful, fantastic time, and I've shagged the brains out of so many of your horny countrymen. Tell him I'll be back to finish bonking the other half of the country next year.'

The man translated to his friends, who roared with laughter. 'Tenga un viaje seguro,' he said, 'Have a safe journey home.'

The first man spoke again. 'Y puede el superior de su lista cuanda ud vuelve para terminar su trabajo bueno?'

'He says, "when you return to finish the good work you are doing, can he be top of your list of names?"'

'Tell him from me,' said Sharon, 'that I'm looking for someone with a prick the size of a donkey and not someone like him, with the brains of a donkey.'

There was silence, and then more laughter as the man realised he'd met his match at last.

FOURTEEN

A SEASON'S GREETING

Dave had just opened for the lunchtime session when Alf the caretaker came in with something rolled up under his arm.

'Bit early for you ain't it, Alf?' asked Dave, placing a pint glass under the bitter tap, Alf's usual tipple.

'No, no – don't pour me one out, I'm just going around the shops asking if they'd stick these posters up for me.' Alf unfolded one and showed Dave who read it out loud.

THE COMMUNITY CENTRE'S CHRISTMAS PARTY DISCO, 23 DECEMBER, 6.30 P.M. UNTIL LATE. VISIT FATHER CHRISTMAS IN SANTA'S GROTTO. RAFFLE, GAMES FOR THE CHILDREN. MUSIC, LATE BAR, ADMISSION – £1 ON THE DOOR. TICKETS IN ADVANCE FROM ALF THE CARETAKER OR FROM BEHIND THE BAR AT THE TAVERN.

'Yeah, sounds good,' said Dave. 'Leave me half a dozen. I'll stick a couple up in the front window and I'll put the rest up around the pub where people can see them.'

'Seeing as you've started pouring that pint, I might as well have it,' said Alf checking his watch. 'I'll take my break now. I ain't stopped since six o'clock this morning, I didn't even have time for a cup of tea, I had that bleedin' idiot Terry on the phone first thing this morning complaining that there was no lights in either lifts over in his block. The way he carries on you'd think he was the only tenant on the whole of the estate. He expects me to wait on him hand and bleedin' foot.'

'This one's on me,' said Dave, knowing how hard Alf worked to keep the estate clean, and how hard he tried to help everyone get along with one another – hence this idea for the Christmas party. The phone rang behind the bar and Dave answered it.

'Hello,' said the voice on the other end, 'can I a speaka to the loveleea bootifulla Wendy? I miss making love to her so much since she go home to England.'

'Get fucked, mate,' said Dave and he put the phone down. 'Whoever's doing that is getting on my nerves now. It's happening at least half a dozen times a day now. When I first started getting the calls, like a dope I thought they were for real. I even asked Wendy what the hell was going on and what had she been playing at while she'd been away. It took me a couple of weeks to realise it was a wind-up but I'm still not sure who the bastard is. He calls himself 'the great Alfredo'. I'll give him fucking Alfredo when he gets my fist in his eye and my toe up his arse.'

'I see they've arrested someone for the murder of that junkie,' said Alf, taking a sip of his beer, and then licking the froth from his lips as he managed to get off the wind-up about Wendy's Spanish lover.

'Funny you should say that. I had the bird who used to live with him in here the other day asking if there was any bar-work going.'

'You'd be skint within a week, with that devious little cow behind the bar. You could trust her to rob you left, right and centre.'

'I did hear,' said Dave, 'that she was arrested the morning after the shooting but was only held for a couple of hours before she was released without charge.'

'Strange carry-on, that,' said Alf.

'Well apparently he had enough people after him,' continued Dave. 'He'd upset that Hell's Angels gang that he used to ride with, plus he sold a dodgy bit of gear to that schoolgirl who collapsed on the playing field the other week.'

'That's right,' said Alf. 'I remember the ambulance picking her up and taking her to hospital.'

'I did hear her father was out for revenge,' said Dave. 'And they ain't the sort of family you'd want to upset or mess with. They've got connections over the East End. Her dad was in here one night with these twins who looked a right handful. They'd done a bit of boxing by the looks of it.'

'Plus they never paid any rent,' said Alf.

Dave laughed. 'The council's hardly going to send round a hit-man to shoot someone who ain't paid their rent are they?'

Alf looked at Dave unable to work out what was so funny. 'Yeah, I suppose you've got a point.' Alf finished his pint and went back off to work.

Over the subsequent weeks the tickets for the Christmas party sold well and with just two days to go it was a complete sell-out. Alf got to work, sticking all the balloons and decorations up, and one of Mr Singh's suppliers dropped off a large Christmas tree which Alf and his fellow roped-in helpers decorated with fairy lights and tinsel. By the time Alf had finished the place looked like Lapland. He'd even built a grotto where the kids could go in and sit on Santa's lap and tell him what they wanted for Christmas. Dave and a couple of his staff from the pub came over and set the bar up, so with only one day to go, everything was ready and in its place.

The big day arrived and after he'd finished his rounds, Alf went over and unlocked the Community Centre. He was standing admiring his own work when the man doing the disco turned up and started to set up his equipment and do a sound check.

'One–two, one–two, one–two,' he repeated into the mike.

'For fuck's sake mate, do us a favour and shut up, you're giving me a headache,' said Alf. The DJ shrugged his shoulders, put down the mike and switched off his equipment.

Lil from the bakers was doing the teas and coffees, so she came in and filled up the tea urn and laid the food out onto a couple of tables. 'I hope you ain't upset him,' she said to Alf. 'We don't want him packing his gear up and going off – where would we get another disco this late in the day?'

'Fuck him,' said Alf, lifting the tinfoil covering a plate of cheese and pickle sandwiches and helping himself to one. 'I'm fucking starving,' he said, stuffing half a sandwich into his mouth. 'I haven't eaten since this morning.'

'That's your lot,' said Lil. 'Them sandwiches and sausage rolls are for the people coming tonight, not for you, you greedy old git.'

Alf apologised but when Lil had turned her back he nicked another one.

'I saw that!' she shouted from the other side of the hall. 'I'll chop your fucking hands off.' People began queuing outside the hall at about 6 p.m. One of Dave's regulars from the pub, Big Joe, had volunteered to dress up as Father Christmas and he turned up with his outfit hidden in a suitcase. Alf showed him to a small room next to the gent's toilets where he could get changed. He told Alf it was a bit early, so he was going to hang his stuff up and go over to the Tavern to have a few pints to get a bit of Dutch courage. Mr Singh arrived with the presents for the kids to go in Joe's sack, all wrapped up in Christmas paper by Mrs Singh. He also had a cardboard box full of prizes for the raffle. He had kindly donated bottles of whisky, vodka and gin, some red and white wine, a box of chocolates, a bottle of perfume for the ladies and a box of the finest Cuban cigars for the men. The doors opened and the first people filed in. Alf stood on the door in his dark-blue suit with white frilly shirt and black dicky-bow collecting the tickets.

'You look smart, Alf, is that the demob suit you got when you left the army?' asked old Fred as he limped past to use the loos.

'Actually, it's not,' replied Alf 'I bought this suit for my daughter's wedding a few years ago and it shows I haven't put on any weight because it still fits.' He unbuttoned the jacket and put his hand inside the waistband and pulled at the top of the trousers, 'plenty of room in there, old son.'

'You look lovely, Alf,' said his wife Dolly. 'Stop worrying. You know old Fred's only trying to get you at it, and winding you up.' Alf smiled. His wife was right – ignore the silly old fool.

The hall soon began to fill up and lots of people were soon out on the dance floor. Alf had to shoo away a couple of the O'Hara kids who were under the Christmas tree trying to peel back the wrapping on the presents to have a peek at what was inside. Mrs O'Hara, along with her husband and one of her sons came in. Alf welcomed them and asked to see their tickets, just like he'd done with everyone else.

'Me granny's got them,' said the son. 'She'll be over with me granddad in a minute.' Alf gave them the benefit of the doubt and let them in.

'I see the Pakis are here,' said Mrs O'Hara loudly, pointing at Mr Singh as he put out a large pot of home-made chicken curry and rice on the food table along with some still warm home-made vegetable samosas.

'You wouldn't catch me eating that shit,' said Mr O'Hara, lifting the lid up and looking inside. 'Jesus fucking Christ, that shit fucking stinks,' he said, slamming the lid back down. 'What the fuck do they put in that shit?'

'Looks like cat- or dog-meat to me,' said Billy Boy, lifting the lid back up again to have another look inside.

'Can I get you some?' asked a smiling Mrs Singh.

'No, not for me love, I don't think my stomach could take it,' replied Billy Boy.

Mr Singh smiled politely. 'It's only a mild chicken curry. It's spicy but not too hot – you should try some.'

'No, not for me, I'm a meat-and-two-veg man,' said Mr O'Hara.

The O'Haras pushed their way to the front of the bar and noisily demanded a drink. 'Come on, mate,' said Billy Boy, waving a fiver under one of the bar-staff's noses, 'we've been here half an hour. Jesus we'll all die of thirst if you don't pull ya finger out!' The bloke behind the bar took no notice and served someone else. 'Jesus he must be fucking deaf as well as stupid,' said Billy Boy, moving along through crowds of people to get right to the middle of the bar to ensure he'd be next.

His gran and granddad appeared at the main door and Alf asked to see their tickets. Gran opened her purse and looked inside. She then checked her coat pockets.

'Did I give them to you?' she asked her husband. He shook his head and checked his pockets. 'I must've left them at home,' she said. 'I'll get Billy Boy to run back and get them.' She looked into the crowded hall and scanned the faces until she spotted Billy Boy still by the bar waving his fiver about, claiming that he was next. Gran shoved him in the back and he looked around.

She whispered something in his ear, took the fiver off him and he walked off out of the hall.

'Any fear of me getting served? I've been here for ages,' said Granny O'Hara, waving the fiver under Dave's nose.

'You'll have to wait patiently like everyone else,' said Dave as he served somebody else. 'Fuck you an' all,' she replied.

Billy Boy passed Tony and Justin on their way into the hall.

'Evening, ladies,' he said sarcastically. 'Any chance of the first dance with one of you when I get back?'

'Tramp,' Justin said.

'Take no notice of them,' said Alf, taking their tickets from them. 'Them O'Hara's could start a fight in an empty room. Just think of it – I fought in the war for the likes of them.' Just as he said that old Fred struggled past on his way to the gents' toilet.

'And he's wearing the suit to prove it!' he laughed.

'Fuck off, peg-leg,' said Alf.

'Bollocks,' came the reply.

'Tell them about the time you were fighting the Germans in the trenches and you came under fire and a bullet entered your head just above your ear and came out just below your knee and the only thing that was damaged was your leg.' Alf started laughing as Tony and Justin looked away, trying not to laugh.

'What the hell did you know about the war?' said Fred. 'You weren't in a proper regiment like the Paras – you were in some regiment like the Long-Range Snipers or the Catering Corps – about a hundred miles away from any action, so get fucked you dwarf.'

'Bollocks.'

'Bollocks to you too.'

Billy Boy soon returned and Alf stood in his way, blocking him from entering the hall. Alf held his hand out. 'Can I see your tickets please?'

'I can't find them,' he said. 'I've searched me Gran's house from top to bottom and I can't find them. She must have lost them somehow.'

Alf wasn't 100 per cent sure that they'd bought tickets in the first place. 'Seeing as it's Christmas I'll take your word for it and let you in,' he said.

Billy Boy walked in as Alf stepped to one side. Standing just inside the door was the rest of his clan. His gran looked at him and winked. The DJ was playing the former number one hit 'Sugar Sugar' by The Archies. The place was really buzzing with a mass of sweaty bodies doing their thing out on the dance floor. Alf did a quick ticket check and worked out that they had a full house. He decided to go to the bar and have a well-earned drink. Dave poured him a pint and brought it over to him.

'Have you seen Big Joe?' asked Alf. 'Only it's getting a bit late for the kids.'

'The last time I saw him he was in the Tavern having a few beers,' said Dave. 'Not to worry he'll turn up. You know what he's like, he's always late. Look at that time when we had the pub's beano down to Southend, he held us all up and was the last one to get back on the coach. He said he'd fallen asleep in a Chinese restaurant – he had the noodles in his hair to prove it.'

Alf looked at his watch. 'As long as he don't let us down – there's 50 kids here who all want to get a present off Santa.'

'No, he'll be here, he's been looking forward to it,' said Dave and he called Wendy over. 'Have you seen Big Joe?'

'I saw him earlier in the pub but I can't say I've noticed him in here,' she replied. Wendy asked Lynn and Sharon who had just come in and were standing at the bar if they had seen him on their travels.

'We've not been here long,' said Lynn.

'You know her,' said Sharon, 'always late.'

'When you've got three kids there ain't enough time in the day for yourself. I've had to get them three bathed and ready for bed, then I've got to get meself bathed and dressed and do me hair and put me make-up on, and then wait for me mum to come over to babysit.'

The DJ played 'I Can't Get No Satisfaction' by the Rolling Stones and dedicated it to Lynn. He looked over and smiled.

'Cheeky git,' she laughed.

'I think he fancies you,' said Sharon.

'I don't even know him.'

'Yes you do, he did the football team's disco in the pub,' said Sharon, waving and smiling back at him. 'If you don't want him, I'll have him.'

'Oi, you're a married woman,' said Lynn.

'Not for much longer. As soon as that wanker comes out of prison me and him are history, and this time I mean it.'

'What about when he starts asking where the money is?'

' "What money," I'll say, "I've spent it." '

'You must have some of it left.'

'Don't forget, I paid for you and me to go to Spain out of it.'

'I said I'd pay you back.'

'I don't want it back.'

'Then why did you mention it?'

'The March of The Mods' came on and the girls went out onto the dance floor. Lynn had only been out there a few seconds when she felt a tap on the shoulder, she looked behind her.

'Hello Lynn, how are you? Do you mind if I join you?'

She looked at the man standing in front of her. 'Who's that?' asked Sharon out the corner of her mouth. Lynn stopped dancing, and looked closely.

'It's me!' said the man.

'Fucking hell!' shrieked Lynn, 'I didn't recognise you.'

'Well, don't keep me in the dark, who is it?' said Sharon still trying to work out who the man was.

'It's Terry,' Lynn said.

'Terry, who?' said Sharon.

'Terry the cabbie,' said Lynn, letting out another shriek of laughter.

'Oh yeah, so it is,' said Sharon, bursting into a nervous giggle. Standing in front of them, hardly recognisable, was indeed Terry the cab driver, he had cut his hair and restyled it into a neat short-back-and-sides. All gone was the pushed-back Brylcreemed look, he'd had a shave and smelt of expensive aftershave. He had on a smart navy-blue mohair suit with a white shirt and black pencil-thin tie. Gone too were the brown, smelly battered desert boots, which had been replaced by a pair of smart, black leather-soled lace-up brogues. The whole transformation was topped off with a little pair of wire-framed, round specs with purple lenses.

'Can I get you ladies a drink?' he asked. They stood there open-mouthed.

'Terry, I'll still can't believe it's really you,' said Lynn. 'You look so different.'

'What's brought all this dramatic change on?' asked Sharon, as more people gathered round to see what all the fuss was about.

'I just felt it was time for a change,' said Terry. 'One day when you've got time, I tell you and Lynn the whole story.' Both girls kissed him and told him how wonderful he looked and he dragged them off to the bar for a drink.

Dave had to look twice because he thought he was seeing things. 'Fuck me, Tel, what's happened?' he said.

Justin came over and shook his hand and asked if he was pleased with his new look. 'Thanks for doing me barnet,' Terry said to him.

'No problem, I'm only too glad to have cut your hair,' said Justin. 'You look a new man, and if I wasn't with Tony, your luck could well be in.'

'Oi – enough of that, I ain't into none of that game.'

'Come on Terry and let's have a dance,' said Sharon, grabbing him by the hand as the sound of James Brown had the dance floor filling up. Earl and his dad got into the middle of the floor and strutted their stuff too.

'You've got to give it to them darkies, they have got a natural rhythm,' said Sharon, as she and Terry made way for their superior footwork and stood back at the bar with Lynn.

'I've never slept with a black man,' said Lynn.

'They do say they've got big winkles,' said Sharon, closely watching Earl and his dad gyrating their hips to the beat of Desmond Decker's 'Israelites'.

'God only gave them big winkles as an apology for fucking their hair up,' said Billy Boy, as he pushed his way through the crowded dance floor to get to the bar. He came back with a tray of drinks and headed towards the table where the rest of the O'Haras were sitting.

'Oi, sambo, calm down!' he laughed as he passed Earl.

Earl stopped dancing 'What's your problem?' he said, clenching his fists by his side and taking a step forward. 'I've had enough shit off you Pikey scumbags with your racial taunts and snide remarks. This time you, or anyone else for that matter, ain't going to get away with it.'

Billy Boy put the tray down in front of his family and turned and faced Earl. 'Now what's your problem nigger-boy?' The two dads on hearing what was going on jumped in-between their warring sons, 'Step out of me way,' said Billy Boy to his father. 'I've had enough of Jimmy Hendrix here and I'm gonna teach him some manners and respect.' Winston's wife stepped forward and gave her son a calming smile and placed a supportive hand on her husband's shoulder.

Alf came over and ordered the O'Haras to drink up and leave.

'We've done nothing wrong,' protested Mr O'Hara. 'I think you'll find it's these jungle-bunnies here that seem to have a problem, and if you ask me they've got chips on their shoulders. All we've done is sit here and have a quiet drink and your man here wants to pick a fight with my son – who, by the way, has done nothing wrong either.'

'It's never you, is it?' said Alf. 'It's always someone else's fault. Go on, get out and don't come back. You shouldn't be in here anyway.'

'What do you mean?' asked Mr O'Hara.

'You and your family never had tickets in the first place and as usual you've conned your way into something for nothing.'

'I don't like your tone,' said Mr O'Hara, towering over Alf menacingly.

'Good,' said Alf, 'and I don't like your face.'

'I'll be reporting you to the council on Monday morning,' Mr O'Hara retorted.

'Good. Now get out.' He nearly said 'before I throw you out', but he didn't want to push his luck.

'Well done, Alf,' said Dave as he came from behind the bar to see what was going on.

'They spoil it for everyone,' said Alf, relieved that none of the O'Haras had taken a swing at him.

'Anyone seen Big Joe?' Dave asked a group of the football team near the bar.

'I ain't seen him since the other night when he was in the pub and he threatened to punch that posh bloke Giles. Apparently Joe was well pissed and he got the posh bloke mixed up with the local child molester and Joe told him he wasn't welcome in the pub and if he didn't leave then Joe would punch his lights out,' said one of the group.

'He was not long ago sitting at the bar over in the Tavern talking to your Kerry,' said another. Dave thought for a second. A terrible image of two people in bed under his roof flashed into his mind. No, he thought, not even Kerry would stoop that low.

The DJ stopped the music and made an announcement over the microphone. 'Ladies and gentlemen, boys and girls, I've heard from a reliable source that in about ten minutes time Santa should be here with us.' A big cheer went up.

Nigel put his coat on. 'I'm going for a walk, Mum . . . Mum? Mum? Are you awake?'

'Oh – I must have dozed off,' she said, opening her eyes. 'Just shows you the rubbish they put on that telly if it makes you go off to sleep like that.'

'I don't know if you heard me but I'm going to pop out for half an hour and get a bit of fresh air. Will you be all right?'

'I'll be all right. It's you I worry about,' she replied.

'I'll be fine. There shouldn't be anyone about, and everyone will probably be over at that Christmas party at the community centre.'

'All right,' she said, 'take care.'

The local anger and ill feeling towards Nigel had subsided a little over the past few weeks and things seemed to have quietened down. The last incident was quite a bad one and it had happened one evening as he carried some groceries home from Mr Singh's shop. A group of lads had seen him go in, waited until he came out and then followed him towards his home. The main group had followed at a discreet distance whilst two of their mates circled around him on their bikes. 'You fucking nonce,' said one. Nigel had felt like pushing him off his bike when he came within reach but thought better of it; he knew what the repercussions were likely to be. The kid had to have been no older than thirteen but what a mouth he had on him.

'You're nothing but a low-life cunt.' Nigel's blood was boiling. The kid continued. 'You lay one finger on me and touch me, and my Dad will get hold of you and kill you.'

Nigel carried on walking. A bottle of milk sailed over his head and smashed on the pavement in front of him. Nigel stopped and turned around. The gang stopped dead in their tracks.

'Lee, ride home and get ya dad,' shouted one of the crowd on a bike.

Nigel felt like saying, 'Yeah – go on Lee, go and get your dad while I wait right here,' but he thought better of it and instead he walked off at a brisk pace. He reached his block and went in through the front doors. He seemed to have lost the kids, or else they'd got fed up and found something else to get up to. He would have taken the stairs but one of the caretakers was mopping them down. The smell of bleach in hot water reminded him of his time in prison. He got into the lift and pressed the button for his floor on the panel on the wall. The doors slid shut and the lift went up. He watched the light above the door flick on indicating where he was as he passed each floor. The lift stopped and the doors slid noisily open. He stepped out and standing in front of him was a kid holding a plastic bucket. The kid had this huge grin spread across his

184

whole face. It reminded Nigel of going to the circus as a young child when the clowns with their painted faces and red sticking-up hair and oversized feet would encourage the kids to smell the flowers pinned on the lapels of their jackets and as they bent down they'd squirt water into the kids faces. Another old trick was pretending to throw a bucket of water onto the children in the front rows, but as they threw it the water turned out to be ripped-up paper and no one got wet and the kids howled with laughter.

This bucket was not so funny. Whoosh – it hit Nigel straight in the face. It took him a few seconds to realise what it was that was running down his face and through his hair, and dripping down his neck and onto his back. Nigel held the arm of his jacket to his nose and breathed in. Straight away he could smell it was piss. It turned out the dirty bastards had all peed in a bucket and had saved it until they'd seen him out and then let him have it.

Shivering at this memory, Nigel came out of the front of the flats and looked around checking the coast was in fact clear. The sound of loud, thumping music drifted across the estate from the party in the community centre. It sounded like Elvis was singing about being 'all shook up'. Nigel pulled his collar up on his jacket to keep the cold wind out. Fish-and-chip wrappers blew across the road. Drinks cans rattled in the kerb. Nigel walked past the fish-and-chip shop which was unusually empty. George the owner sat behind the counter on a wooden stool, looking out of the window bored out of his brains, having a fag and blowing smoke rings into the air, knowing that in a few hours' time the place would be packed with hungry revellers only too eager to hand their money over so they could fill their rumbling tums with greasy fish and chips.

THE ESTATE

He walked past the pub and looked in through the window. It was empty except one old boy propping up the bar, holding a Brown and Mild with his yellow nicotine-stained fingers, a dog-end hanging from his lip. Nigel thought about going in – he hadn't had a pint of beer for ages. He pulled his hand from his jacket pocket and tugged at the door. The old boy looked around and Kerry looked up from the newspaper she was reading which was spread out across the bar. He changed his mind at the last second and walked away from the pub. He carried on walking and in the darkness he could see a figure up ahead of him. Whoever it was was swaying and staggering as he or she walked along, whoever it was was having difficulty walking in a straight line. The person was going two steps forward and two steps back and then would stop and cling on to the wing of a parked car to keep upright. Nigel could now see it was Big Joe.

'You all right mate?' asked Nigel, realising he was well pissed. Joe struggled to say anything, as he couldn't seem to get his mouth to work. Nigel could smell booze on his breath and by the looks of it, he'd pissed his trousers. 'Come on mate, I'll help you get home.'

Joe didn't have a clue who was trying to help him. Nigel put his shoulder under Joe's shoulder and his arm around his waist.

'Wait, *waaitt*,' stuttered Joe, spit and foam forming in each corner of his mouth. 'Don't take me home, take me to the *community* centre.'

'I think you should be going home and not having any more to drink,' said Nigel. 'It looks as though you've had enough.'

'Noo – nooo, no, listen to me,' said Joe, a hint of aggression in his voice, 'just take me to the community centre OK?' Nigel struggled along with the weight of Joe and somehow got him to the main doors. Sitting outside, propped up against the wall in a right old state, with sick all down his front and over his leather jacket, was the boy who had accused Nigel of making lurid remarks to him, a member of the gang that chased him into the river over the park. He was nearly unconscious and was groaning and moaning as he tried to get to his feet. His hands were splayed out next to him. Nigel looked about, checked there was no one around and trod on his fingers, putting his whole weight as well as Joe's onto the kid's hand. He could hear flesh tearing and human bones creaking and snapping as the fingers ground into the pavement. The kid looked up, exhilarating pain registering and spreading across his face. His mouth opened wide but no words came out as he coughed, and spewed up more beer and food. Nigel struggled through the double doors with Joe.

'Sorry, mate,' said Nigel to the kid and made out that it was Joe who'd trod on his fingers. 'Come on, Joe, you've got to be more careful. You could have hurt that young man.'

Joe pointed across the corridor. 'Up here, up here,' he mumbled. Nigel edged along with Joe, now almost unconscious, on his shoulder. Nigel could see a door open next to the gents' toilets. Joe pointed inside. 'This will do,' he slobbered. Nigel carried him inside and closed the door behind them. He dropped Joe in a heap onto a plastic chair. Hanging up was the Father Christmas outfit which Joe was supposed to be wearing. He looked at Joe who was now already fast asleep and snoring his head off.

'That was absolutely delicious, thank you darling,' said Giles to his wife as he lifted his knife and fork and empty plate from the table and into the stainless-steel sink. 'Have you two kids both finished yours?'

'Thank you, Daddy,' they both said and they asked to leave

the table. Giles sat next to his wife on the sofa as the two kids got engrossed in something on the telly.

'Are you taking the children over to the Christmas party at the centre?'

'Well I wasn't going to,' Giles replied. 'I think it's so ridiculous that someone should arrange a kiddie's party so late at night.'

Giles' wife looked up at the clock on the mantelpiece and smiled. 'It's only eight o'clock now and they haven't got to get up early for school in the morning.'

'No. I'd much rather have an early night tonight and get up at a good hour in the morning and get the car we've borrowed from your mother loaded up so we can be on our way before the roads get busy. As well as asking us to bring the Christmas presents your mum did ask us to bring some chairs with us so that we could all sit around the table for Christmas dinner at the same time. Only there's four of us and she's only got a couple of chairs. I must go downstairs and sort out that old roof rack and that heavy rope we've got buried somewhere in the bike shed.' He jumped to his feet. 'I'll go and do it now while I remember.' He put his coat on and grabbed the car keys. 'I won't be half an hour love.'

'Can I come with you?' Asked one of the girls, bored with what was on telly.

'No. You wait here with Mummy. It's far too cold for you to go out tonight.'

'Oh please.'

'No it's too cold.'

'Cold?' said his wife, puzzled. 'Just an hour ago you were saying how mild it was for this time of the year.'

'I won't be long love,' he said as he slammed the front door shut behind him.

'Ladies and gentlemen, boys and girls,' announced the DJ, 'I'm going to slow things down for you and I'd like all you couples to get up on to the floor and get that bit closer. Here, especially for you, is the sound of Mr Otis Reading and "Sitting on the Dock of the Bay".'

'Would you care to dance?' Terry asked Lynn.

'I'd love to.' She plonked her handbag in Sharon's lap, took Terry's hand and went out onto the dance floor. 'Hold that for us will ya, Shaz?'

'Jammy cow, she gets all the men,' said Sharon to no one in particular. 'She was the same in Spain with all them waiters around her, like flies around a cow's arse.'

'Care to dance?' said the DJ, who had suddenly appeared in front of her.

'Oh yes please,' she said, dumping her and Lynn's bag on the chair next to her.

Terry and Lynn were dancing together, her arms draped around his neck, holding him close. 'So what's with the new image then, Terry?' Lynn asked.

'I just fancied a change that's all.'

'But why?' she asked. 'There must have been a reason.'

'I told you earlier, when you've got the time I'll sit down with you and tell you all about it.' She stopped dancing and looked at him.

'Let's sit down and you can tell me now,' she said, pointing to the chair with her bag on.

'It'll take too long and anyway you can't hear yourself with the music.'

'Let's go somewhere quieter then,' she said as she pulled him towards her and kissed him on the lips. He came up for air, not believing his luck.

'Like where?'

'Your place?' She kissed him again.

'We can't,' he said. 'It's a mess. I haven't hoovered or dusted. How about yours?'

She thought for a minute. 'All right then, but no funny stuff. My mum will be there. She's babysitting for me.' Terry smiled and she kissed him on the cheek.

Lynn grabbed her bag. 'See ya, Sharon, we're off.'

Sharon didn't take a lot of notice, she was too busy seeing what the DJ tasted like. She broke away long enough to take a breath: 'Don't do anything I wouldn't.'

'Well that doesn't leave much,' laughed Lynn.

'Father Christmas is here!' shouted a group of kids. 'Yes, yes – yessss . . . ' they all shouted, jumping up and down with excitement as they spotted Father Christmas coming out of the storeroom carrying his loaded sack.

'Bleeding hell, you're cutting it a bit fine,' said Alf. 'I was beginning to think you weren't turning up.'

'Some organiser you are,' said old Fred, coming out of the toilets, his weak bladder having got the better of him. 'You couldn't organise a piss-up in a brewery.' The pair of them squared up to one another.

'Come on, you short-arsed git,' said Fred, taking up a fighting stance like an old-fashioned prizefighter. 'I'll knock your block off!'

'Come on, you cripple,' said Alf, keeping his guard up and bobbing up and down on the spot.

Dave butted in. 'Gentlemen, please control yourselves. We have more pressing issues to think about than watching two old codgers knock ten bails of shit out of one another.'

'Two old codgers? You cheeky bastard . . . ' said Fred and Alf, united for a split second in a temporary truce.

'Alf, you silly old fool, just what do you think you are doing?' asked his wife, pushing him in the chest. 'You're meant to be organising the Father Christmas grotto.'

All the kids were patiently lined up as Father Christmas, his hood pulled over his head, sat each child in turn on his lap and asked them if they'd been a good boy and girl and what they would like for Christmas.

'Alf!' shouted his wife. 'One of the kids at the back of the queue has been sick. Can you go and get a mop and bucket and clear it up?'

'Can't someone else do it?' Alf replied, 'like the child's mother for instance? All I seem to do is clear up everyone else's mess. I seem to spend my whole life carrying around a mop and a bucket of soapy water.'

'That's what caretakers do,' said his wife.

Alf tutted and went off to get the bucket and a mop. He came back almost immediately. His face was as white as a sheet – as if he'd seen a ghost. Standing behind him with his wrists bound together with a thick rope was Big Joe.

'I think we have an impostor amongst us,' Alf said as he moved the kids to one side and whipped Father Christmas's false white beard from his face.

'Aha – got ya!'